Not A Lesser Happiness

Doug Stewart

An Even Money Book
Los Angeles

Even Money Press
Los Angeles

evenmoney.press

First edition. May 2017.
ISBN 978-0-9962204-6-0

For Laughs

Not A Lesser Happiness

To me she speaks; she moves me for her theme.
What, was I married to her in my dreams?
Or sleep I now, and think I hear all this?
What error drives our eyes and ears amiss?
Until I know this sure uncertainty,
I'll entertain the offered fallacy.
The Comedy of Errors.
Shakespeare

1

THIS IS HOW IT BEGINS

This happened to me up at that deli just off Beverly Glen, up by Mulholland. It's like a Jewish deli back East. Got all this Jewish comfort food. So I'd ordered and I was sitting at one of the tables outside waiting for my breakfast when this good looking couple approached me and asked if I'd mind if they sat with me. "With me?" and I turned to look at the other tables, which were all full. "Place is really busy," the guy said. "So we were wondering if we could share." And I was all alone at my large table, one that really was more appropriate for four, but I always sit outside, and when I can at that table, so I sort of felt proprietary, like, but this is my table, but I just shrugged and pointed to the empty chairs. "Help yourself," I said. Then once they were seated the guy leaned over to say "X," as he shook my hand. I'm calling him X because if I used his real name most of you would know who I'm talking about, although at the time I had no idea who he was. "And this is "Y," he said, introducing his companion, and I shook her hand as well. And again, even though her name meant nothing to me it most likely would to you.

"Come here often?"

"I used to," he said. "How about you?"

"Me?" I shrugged. "Mostly during the week. Today I was thinking about Joan's over in Studio City, but they do this farmer's market every Sunday so—"

"You live over there?"

"In Studio City? No. Actually, I live just down the hill." I was pointing down Beverly Glen towards Bel Air. "And you?"

"Off Roscomare. Stradella?" I nodded, I knew Stradella, that's one of my favorite shortcuts up from UCLA to Mulholland. Very pricey. What I subsequently learned—and this from her—was that he owned one of those places they'd rebuilt after the big Bel Air-Brentwood fire of 1961. When most of those homes were burned right down to the slab: wind whipped embers, shake shingle roofs, brush down in the canyons.

"So this is close."

"Close, and there's not much else up here."

"There's always the Valley."

"Or Beverly Hills," she said.

"Too many paparazzi."

I smiled. "Never had that problem."

"See," she said, sounding like she worked for *Access Hollywood*, "celebrities are just like the rest of us. Out for breakfast in Bel Air."

"You don't mean here?" I said, sitting up like I should have a good look around.

"There," she said, looking at him. "What'd I tell you?"

I smiled at her. "Oh, and what was that?"

"That you'd have no idea who we were," he said. "Not that it matters, since according to her no one does."

"Hurts his feeling," she said, patting his hand.

"Sorry, but then I could be surrounded by celebrities and never even know it."

"Eating here, you probably are," he said.

"And you?" I asked, looking at her. "I suppose this means you're a *someone* too?"

"Well . . ."

"What do you mean, well?" he said. "Of course you are. Name recognition. A trusted brand."

"Yes, if only I were as popular with the critics as I am with my fans."

"And don't forget all those cars you've sold," he teased. "Now, if we could only get you to buy one."

"Seriously? You live in Los Angeles and you don't own a car? How is that even possible?"

"Oh, it's possible," she said. "But mostly it's inconvenient."

So they did order, and I hung around eating slowly as they caught up. They were fun. Then when he got up to use the restroom she said to me: "So, Mort, what do you do?" No, of course my name isn't Mort, that's just the name I'd given them, and no, I have no idea why I'd felt like I needed to do that.

"I'm a writer."

"Ah," she said, settling back in her chair.

"You mean I shouldn't be?"

"No, it's just that I've never found writers to be very trustworthy."

Trustworthy? Writers? You mean someone actually thought we were? So I said: "I hardly know what to say. I guess I've never been in a position to judge. But I take it you have?"

"Unfortunately."

"Sorry."

"No need to be, not unless you write for one of those TV shows. You don't, do you?"

I shook my head. "No, I write mysteries, which so far have failed to capture the attention of anyone but my loyal readers." I'd written four, plus some other stuff I think is much better, though no one else seems to think so.

"I read mysteries. Maybe I've read one of yours."

"It's possible." Actually, it was more than possible since even though I tend to sneer at them they remain wildly popular.

"So what are they?"

"They're about this guy who used to be a cop only now he's retired. Actually, he was injured on the job and now he's on disability. Well, it's not much. I mean it never is, is it? So he lives in his RV and travels around the country staying in different RV parks. And here's the weird part, because no matter where he stays you can always count on trouble making an appearance."

"Presenting him with another mystery."

"What little mystery there is, since it's really more about him and how he sees his world, the places where he hangs his hat, the people he encounters."

"Psychological, not procedural."

"You might say that." I had said that, many times, while looking for a publisher.

"And the titles?"

"Yeah, titles . . ." and here I was really stuck because one peek at Amazon and not only would she see I was no

Mort, she'd have all the proof she needed that I was just another untrustworthy writer.

"Wow, so reluctant," she said, watching me. "I guess that means you really aren't a writer. Or maybe you just don't write mysteries."

"No, I write them."

"You do? Because I was beginning to think you wrote something silly like self-help books and were just too embarrassed to tell me."

"I would be too embarrassed to tell you."

"And Mort?"

"Yeah, good old Mort."

"So?"

"Sorry, I have no idea why I said that. Maybe celebrities intimidate me."

"Though you're quickly getting used to us."

"So it would seem." So I told her the names of my books. "The first one, that's *Point Panic,* then *Quartzite Moonrise, Sedona Slay Ride*—"

"S-l-a-y?"

"Afraid so."

"And?"

"And now my latest, *Yuma Me,* and yes, that's Y-u-m-a."

"And the author of these fine books would be?"

"Frosty."

"Frosty!"

"After the snowman—I think—since I've never been able to get a straight answer out of my parents."

"Well," she said, shaking her head, "definitely a writer."

"Sorry. Maybe you should make that a screwdriver." I was nodding at her orange juice. "If this isn't too early in the morning for you."

"Not today."

Then X was back, telling us as he sat down about running into a couple of actors he knew sitting inside who were complaining about the lack of work and, well, it was the sort of conversation I just tune out. Then she said, "So old Mort here is a writer. Mysteries," and then she looked at me and grinned, which I appreciated, her polite complicity in my little white lie. So I told him what I'd told her, but omitting those embarrassing titles, which was fine, his curiosity about me only went so far, which, unlike hers, wasn't very far at all. So breakfast was finished, they thanked me again for letting them share my table, and I told them it was my pleasure, though I was sorry we'd missed those paparazzi. How I'd really been looking forward to seeing myself in *People Magazine*, which amused them. Then they left, but I made sure to see what he was driving. Of course, a red Ferrari Italia, and *of course* because only in L.A. will you see people running errands in cars that cost a quarter of a million dollars. Not that it bothers me to see that sort of thing because it doesn't. I like cars. I'm sure I'd do the same if I had the money.

2

YOU'RE JUST WINGING IT, AREN'T YOU?

So I guess I should jump ahead a bit and explain that Y—and let's just call her Cyd—got her agent to track me down, then surprised me by calling to say how much she enjoyed my books even though she was a bit taken aback by how dark they were. She said with those titles she was expecting something more carefree. Then she got curious about my next one. "There is a next one, isn't there?" And I told her, "Yes, though it's sort of stalled at the moment." What I wanted to say was, yes, unfortunately, but wouldn't you rather read some of my other stuff? But then this is the problem I always have, that even though people are eager to hear all about John Esposito and those RV park murders, none of that same eagerness ever seems to extend to my more *serious* fiction. So we agreed to meet over in Brentwood at Caffe Luxxe, which is on 26th Street not far from where she was staying in this swanky guesthouse on Bristol. Yes, I'd bring along my laptop. That's how she ended up reading this:

> One of the reasons he liked the desert was the pain, that deep in the bone ache he often got in the middle of the night that forced him to get up and hobble around until it eased. For that, the dry heat was a balm, but then so was a drink or two, but no pills, he'd rather be an alcoholic than get addicted to those damn pills the

doctors were always pushing on him. So hot and dry was his preference, and it didn't get much hotter anywhere than along the Colorado River. Yes, Death Valley, but that was a national park, no semi-permanent guests allowed, and then there was that name. No, not interested. But just how hot did he want it? Like three years ago when he'd just missed that 128 in Lake Havasu City, though it had still managed to hit 122 downriver where he was staying in that RV park in Parker. So, yes, even for him it could get too hot, which is why he'd started heading for the coast or the mountains to ride it out until the monsoon season arrived to shade things a bit. This year, for example, he was sitting it out up at Julian over in California, while two years ago he'd spent a chilled-to-the-bone summer driving up and down the coast from Oregon to San Diego staying in state campgrounds. Beautiful, but just too cold, they never let you stay very long, the amenities were shabby or nonexistent, and he didn't much care for the stoners or surfers, two groups that were pretty much congruent so far as he could tell.

He'd met the Gustafsons last spring in Borrego. Now that was nice, a little bit of middle-class suburbia way out there in the desert like San Diego had an outpost. Now they were texting him about a nice park in Calexico. The border right there, friendly folks, cheap rent, good food. Good food? He knew what that meant. American style buffets. Cheap, all-you-can-eat Chinese places. But maybe it also meant Mexican. Farmacias? Yes, drug prices would be much cheaper just across the border in Mexicali. Maybe he should check it out.

It wasn't all that surprising he'd fallen in with an older crowd. After all, that's who snowbirds were, that, and mostly affluent, mostly white, mostly from the upper Midwest or Canada, and mostly just wanting to spend winter someplace sunny and warm. They were well informed, too, finding new places, returning to old favorites, usually en masse. The word would go out: this winter it's Calexico. So they were good company even if they were a bit older, more so than those other groups one often found in the parks: the underclass, the drifters, the chronically unemployable, the druggies, the whacked out loners, the rejects, the outsiders, the losers in Obama's tepid economic recovery.

"What's wrong with Obama?" she asked.

"Nothing. I voted for him, twice, but unless you're working for Goldman Sachs you're still just treading water."

"Well," she said, taking off her glasses, "so far I really like it, but I hope you're not going to kill off more snowbirds."

"The Gustafsons?"

"Because they're probably very nice. Just like my parents."

"Sorry." What could I say? At times the snowbird body count did run a bit high.

"I've never understood why you writers feel like you need to do that. Kill off all these nice people."

"It's no different in the movies."

"I know, death and murder. Surely, you can come up with some other way to show us how serious you are."

"Yes, but in my case they are called *murder* mysteries. Can't have a whodunit if no one's done it."

"*A* murder, yes, but not a slaughter of innocents."

"Oh, I don't think anyone's getting slaughtered, but my readers do expect a bit of just retribution. To set that up, to give them that frisson, my bad guys have to be pretty bad." But she's right, not only does it get tiresome constantly killing people off, it's nothing but a big pain in the ass trying to come up with new ways of doing so. And then the end result is things just get more sadistic and violent, which can't help but have a coarsening effect on one's artistic sensibilities. Right. Like I need to be worried about that. "Take a look at *Sedona Slay Ride*," I said. "It's much lighter in tone than the first two." *Point Panic* and *Quartzite Moonrise*, those were the first two, the two she'd read.

"And this one?" She was tapping my laptop.

"*A Cold Night in Slab City*?"

"Because that title makes it sound rather grim."

"Yes, but Slab City's a place, not a morgue, if that's what you're thinking." I hoped she was, since the whole point of that title was to suggest that double entendre. Sort of like a smart-ass Chandler, calling the morgue *slab city*. Or is that just too pretentious?

"Is it really? Because I've never even heard of it."

"I'm not surprised, it's hardly a major tourist destination, though the Europeans seem to like dropping by."

"Europeans?"

"I think it meets their expectations."

"For?"

"That we're just one small step away from some sort of insane dystopia."

"But you said something about being hung-up on the plot."

"I know, but it's not that so much as it is finding the right tone, setting the proper mood, establishing a strong sense of place."

"So it's not the plot?"

"Honestly, plots aren't that hard, for the most part they're pretty generic, but the details, those take some thought. That's why I've been thinking about Calexico, Mexicali just across the border, how there's got to be all sorts of criminal activity down there to draw upon."

"Like drug cartels?"

"Exactly. I just need to come up with some way of getting that into an RV park."

"And Slab City?"

"Well, Slab City's definitely going to find its way in there at some point." I'd already decided, Slab City was where something bad was going down, I just wasn't sure what that something bad was yet.

"I'm amazed, I thought you guys had this sort of thing all mapped out beforehand, but you're just winging it, aren't you?"

"That's just how I like to work. Spontaneity. Luck. Coincidence. Serendipity. Or maybe it's just my low threshold for boredom."

In case you've been wondering, this is how they go. First up, *Point Panic,* a chronicle of John Esposito's maiden trek in his new RV, one that finds him all the way down in Mexico in Puerto Peñasco (aka Rocky Point) on the Gulf of California. Turns out, that's a pretty rough place for snowbirds. Next, we've got *Quartzite Moonrise,* which takes place up around Quartzite, Arizona, another rough place for snowbirds, though this time it's rampaging biker gangs. That's followed by *Sedona Slay Ride*, which marks a major departure from the desert tales. Seasonal, which my publisher liked, and it sold well, which I certainly liked, but that dust jacket with Esposito's RV all decked out in Xmas shit was a major embarrassment. And now my latest, *Yuma Me*, which finds our hero back in the desert, a much more comfortable setting for both of us, though some of my readers have complained that the story is too dark. Well, perhaps it is, but as far as I'm concerned that's just what we all needed after that lighthearted romp up in Sedona. And now we've come full circle, just treading water while we wait to see what happens with *A Cold Night in Slab City*. But I have to say, I've already fallen in love with the locale: the Salton Sea, the ruins at Bombay Bay, Salton City, Slab City with its sun-crazed artists, El Centro, Calexico with its proximity to the border, that flat landscape, ubiquitous agribusiness, the uneasy mix of two nations and cultures.

I'm thinking this may also be a good time to say a bit more about my protagonist, my retired ex-cop, John Esposito, or Dion, as he's known to his friends. Like how his disability (crushed pelvis) was the result of auguring in during a high-speed pursuit—ran into the back of an illegally parked semi—in a dark and gritty warehouse district in his hometown of Philadelphia. Or how this was followed by many months of mind-numbing convalescence and torturous rehab. Or how he's like most of these fictional detective types: classic loner, divorced, no kids, few friends. All of which is why it comes as no surprise that once he's free of his hellish ordeal all he can think about is getting the fuck out of Dodge. That's when he sells his crappy little condo and his old Camry, buys an RV, and sets out. He's headed west. Doesn't know where, doesn't really care, he just wants to be on the road. It's an American tale.

So the parks tended to self-segregate, everyone settling in among their own cohort. And did they love to socialize, being the lucky heirs of a youth spent growing up in the bucolic middle-class suburbs of the 1950s and 1960s. In fact, they'd always gotten along, pulled together, made a world of their own, the whole huge mass of them. Nothing about that had changed. But he was a bit younger, not young enough to be one of their children, but young enough not to have known their world, not to know it even now. No matter. Their kindness and generosity were boundless. Of course it was that, his otherness, his not really belonging, that had led him to his current state—the cranky but not yet really old loner they took under their wing. In recompense, he brought justice.

"Brought justice?" She looked up at me. "Jesus, Frosty, he kills people."

"Yes, but he's protective."

"Only because of how you make them seem, like they need protecting."

"So now you don't want him protecting those nice Gustafsons?"

"No, but he could be a little less trigger happy."

"I tried that in *Sedona Slay Ride*."

"And?"

"Read it, you'll see." What I'd done, I'd toned down the violence. Come on, it's supposed to be a Christmas story. So no one got shot. Okay, beat-up, run over, hit over the head, sure, lots of that, but no serious mayhem. I thought of it as if they were just a bunch of very bad elves. You don't shoot elves.

Don and Donna Gustafson. How was that possible, those matching names like they were brother and sister? But he was always amazed by stuff like that, ironies, impossible coincidences, by how things could repeat themselves for no apparent reason. Well, cops saw a lot of that, all that inexplicable shit, which is why he often found himself pondering what he took to be the extreme nature of God's sense of humor. How not only did she have one, which for Dion was a given, but how it so often had a mean edge to it. Dark, grimly ironic, but the joke was still there if one looked hard enough. Maybe that's what he ought to do, look in that dark place for the humor in his own life, the hidden joke buried somewhere under all that rubble.

But that sort of thing didn't bother the Gustafsons. Actually, none of those baby boomers seemed particularly given to melancholy or endless reflection. Certainly not like he was, anyway. It was all those drugs they'd done in college, just burned that negativity right out of their heads. He smiled. He was always doing that, contrasting things to his own disadvantage, but that was such bull. He knew, for instance, that Don had been in Nam. Wouldn't really talk about it, but he'd been there. What they did have—a clear advantage over him—was their belief that life had both meaning and purpose. He wasn't so sure about either.

She stopped reading to look at me.

"What?"

"He's certainly getting thoughtful."

"He's always been thoughtful."

"Not like this." She took her glasses off and rubbed the bridge of her nose. "Do you actually know any cops? Because I'd love to know if this is how they really think."

"You don't think they do?"

"I don't see how they could do their jobs if they did."

"I'm sure they'd love to hear you say that. Like they never reflect on what they do. Never worry about making a mistake. Never pay the price for having a guilty conscience."

"Is that where this is headed, Dion's suddenly going to develop a guilty conscience?"

"Develop? He's always had one. I was just thinking it was going to get a bit more existential."

Smiling, she put her hand on my arm. "You do know you're hopeless, don't you?" She was referring to my on-going attempts to get her to read some of my more serious stuff. What I'd done, hoping to intrigue her, was tell her they were sort of French in tone. "You know, more philosophical, labyrinthine, elusive?" Well, no, she really didn't know, so I took a different tack, suggesting they shared a bit of that cool French New Wave magic of the 1960s. "The cinema? Truffaut, Resnais, Goddard?" Nope. "Okay, how about Camus? You have heard of him?" That did it, now she was annoyed. "Where he kills that guy on the beach? We had to read that in high school. But then that would appeal to you."

He liked Calexico. It was bigger than he'd expected, not quite American in every respect, which meant not quite like everywhere else, yet clearly still America. He'd wondered about that, about how much it would be like Mexico, and there were strong similarities, not the least of which was that everyone spoke Spanish, the local lingua franca. So he called the Gustafsons to tell them he was nearly there, and by the time he arrived they were waiting for him at the park office to make sure he signed on for the spot they'd reserved for him next to theirs.

"Frosty?"

"Now what?"

"Sorry, but I was just wondering if you've ever been to Calexico."

"Does it matter?"

"So any local color I might happen to run across, and I know there will be since that seems to be one of your specialties, is just something you've made up?"

"You make it sound like I'm cheating you."

"Not me, your readers. Seriously. Suppose someone reads your book and says, hey, this Calexico sounds like a fun place, maybe we should drive down there for spring break, but when they do it's a big disappointment."

"Come on, who'd be foolish enough to plan their vacation around a murder mystery?"

"But you've had some letters, haven't you?" She was watching me while chewing on the end of her glasses, looking so very thoughtful (and by now I'm sure you're beginning to see just how *very* thoughtful she could be). "From some of your fans, I mean. Asking for information on where to stay and what to do? Because I can see by that look on your face you have. I hope you haven't let them down."

"How? By not writing travelogues?"

"So you just make this stuff up as it suits you? About these places you take us to in your books?"

"I do a bit of research. Google things. Look at Street View."

"All the time, or just when you're stuck?"

"Some of the time."

"You know what I think." And she paused to give me one of her brighter smiles. "We need to drive down there and check it out."

"Calexico?"

"Why not? We could even rent an RV. See if we can't make an honest man of you."

"Uh . . . really, Cyd, I'm not so sure that's such a good idea, just the two of us down there in an RV park. And what about your schedule? I thought you said this was a busy time for you?"

"I've still got a couple of weeks before we start up again."

But it really was a good idea. Certainly not one I would have come up with on my own. But then that's Cyd, a real doer, not one to sit around all day hammering away on her laptop. And an RV was perfect for her, a true reflection of how she preferred to live her life, which was with few possessions and even fewer attachments.

3

LIFE'S TRAVELLERS

RV aren't cheap, renting or buying, and neither are the parks, and then we went back and forth over whether we'd go with a Class A motorhome, which look like buses, or a Class C, which are smaller and have that little extra bit over the cab. Cyd, of course, wanted all the luxury she could get, but since I'd be the driver I preferred something smaller.

"But maybe we should do this like Dion does in your books."

"I don't see why since you seem to believe I just make this stuff up as I go along. Plus, can I just say how weird this is, hearing you talk about Dion like he's a real person."

"It is strange, isn't it? How this imaginary person of yours starts taking on a life of his own."

"Only for you and my readers, because he certainly doesn't for me."

"Sure he does, or else how would you be able to write about him?"

"*About* him?" I just had to sit there a moment shaking my head. "You know, maybe old Arthur Conan Doyle was right, in the end it's better to kill them off."

"But he didn't."

"Oh yes he did, and I bet it felt wonderful."

"But then he brought him back."

"Only because he had to pay the bills."

"Is that true?"

I shrugged. "I don't know. Maybe. It certainly would be in my case."

"Is that why you're being so stubborn about this, because you can't afford it?"

"I can't."

"So let me pay. I might even be able to get the studio to cover some of it. Well, why not? You know I can afford it." Yes, I did know. What they paid her was amazing. I'd really had no idea.

"Thanks. That's a very generous offer. But I think we should just stick to our original agreement to split the cost." Then I laughed. "Ding the studio for an RV trip? How's that possible?"

"Because they usually do cover some of my expenses, though they rarely have to these days since I mostly camp out with friends."

"What they should do is buy you one of those big buses you seem to like so much. See if that might not settle you down."

"I've tried that."

"When?"

"When I used to own a condo in New York."

"You like living like that, don't you? Sans encumbrances."

"And you don't?"

"I have a few things."

"Uh-huh. A car, an apartment, some clothes, some books, it's not much."

"It's enough." That wasn't a lie, though even then I was wondering how I might manage to hang on to her.

Not that anyone ever had. But we'd been together a lot that week. She'd spent a night at my place. I'd spent two with her over in Brentwood. More than enough to stir up what later became a rather profound longing. I know. Hopeless.

"That's probably why we're so simpatico," she said. "Two of life's travelers, both of us traveling light." Well, at that I just had to smile. I mean, not only was it true, it was just one more charming example of her unexpectedly poetic way of expressing herself. "Why are you smiling at me like that?" she asked.

"Because I love how your mind works. How that artist's sensibility keeps rising to the surface. Maybe that's why you became an actor."

"No, it's the money, there's nothing very artistic about acting."

4

THE MINNIE WINNIE AND THE VENUSIANS

In the end, what we did was drive down to San Diego in my car, pick up the RV (Winnebago Minnie Winnie; one year old; 27 footer; Ford F-450 cab; slideout dinette) at a dealer in San Marcos ($1050/week or $155/night; 3 night minimum; additional fees for cookware and bedding; $1000 damage deposit; no charge, 125 miles/day, but $0.35/per each additional mile; free secured parking for my car), and head out. Well, no, what actually happened was the agent spent about an hour with us walking us through all the features, then answering the many questions neophytes like us commonly have.

"How're you doing?" She was watching me as I drove slowly down the freeway.

"Fine, but it's a bit of a challenge." It was, too. The length, the width, the height, you really had to pay attention, in particular when turning a corner, being careful not to turn too tightly, pinching off the nose of a few parked cars or crushing a few pedestrians. All of which made me realize just how much I'd underestimated the skill it took to drive one. Likewise, how much I'd overestimated their maneuverability. Yes, from now on there would be far fewer driving stunts in my books. But why had none of my readers ever complained? There was only one possible answer: like me, they'd never been anywhere near an RV.

"What route is Dion going to take in your book?"

"I'm not sure yet, but I've been thinking it might be fun to have him set out from up at Julian, which means we'll pick up his trail out east in the desert near Ocotillo."

"Well . . ."

"I'm the driver."

"I know. I was just hoping for a bit more . . ."

"Verisimilitude?"

So Julian it was, a place I'd actually been before, I'd even made that drive down to the desert, which is what made me think of it in the first place. Down the Banner Grade to Scissors Crossing and S2, the old Butterfield Overland Mail route past the Butterfield Ranch Resort and Vallecito Stage Stop Park, up and down and over and around the hills, then the desert floor, Ocotillo, and I-8.

But we didn't make it to Julian. My fault. We got started too late, I drove too slowly, traffic was heavy, we stopped to buy groceries in Ramona, and when we called we couldn't find any vacancies, though they did refer us to the nearby Oak Knoll Campground, which is where we spent that first night. It's actually quite lovely, located just where S6 splits off from 76 to make its long twisty way up Palomar Mountain.

She read from their website as I drove. "We have excellent facilities at Oak Knoll Campground. We have pool tables, a playground for the little kids, we also have a WiFi Hot Spot and a small store to purchase snacks, drinks, ice and firewood. You can relax in one of our rental cabins, enjoy a spacious RV site, or pitch your tent in one of our oak groves. This is a terrific place to view the Milky Way or watch for UFOs. In fact, our campground is world famous for being the spot where the first documented UFO encounter took place."

"First documented UFO encounter? What does that mean?" What it meant, we soon discovered, was George Adamski, patron saint of the contactees, whose books we later found prominently displayed in the campground's little store.

"Here we go." She was looking at Wikipedia on her iPhone as I tried to get us backed into our spot (and thank god for that backup camera!). "Born in Poland in 1891. Came to the U.S. with his family when he was two. Died in 1965. And listen to this: from 1913 to 1916, beginning at the age of 22, he was a soldier in the 13th U.S. Cavalry Regiment fighting at the Mexican border during the Pancho Villa Expedition."

"I wonder if he was ever in Calexico?"

"Got married in 1917. No children. Then in the early 1930s he and his wife moved to Laguna Beach where he founded something called the Royal Order of Tibet."

"He was a hustler."

"Well, it was Southern California. It also sounds like they had a temple, the Temple of Scientific Philosophy. And this is interesting, it says that during Prohibition they had a license to make wine."

"For religious purposes only, I'm sure."

"Then in 1940," she stopped reading to look at me. "Are you all right?"

"Why, am I looking a bit flustered? Like maybe it's a hell of a lot harder parking one of these babies than I say in my books?"

"Yes, but now you have."

"Yes, unfortunately now I know. So," I said, sitting back in my captain's chair. "As you were saying."

"That it sounds like they had some sort of cult, because in 1940, Adamski, his wife, and some friends, moved out to a ranch near Palomar Mountain."

"Where we are now."

"I don't think so, because it says in 1944, with the help of one of his students, they purchased 20 acres of land on Palomar Mountain where they built a new home, a campground called Palomar Gardens, and a small restaurant called the Palomar Gardens Cafe."

"So this is the old Palomar Gardens Campground."

"Uh-huh. And then things really got interesting."

"Is that so?"

"Oh, yeah. October 9, 1946, during a meteor shower, Adamski and friends claimed to have witnessed a large cigar-shaped mother ship."

"1946? Here at Palomar Gardens campground? Because that's really early for UFOs." It was, too, since it was Kenneth Arnold's sighting up by Mt. Rainer on June 24, 1947 that started it all.

"The same ship he later claimed to have photographed in 1947 as it crossed in front of the moon."

"Also here at Palomar Gardens?"

"That's right. Then later that same year—"

"1947?"

"1947. When—following the first widely publicized UFO sighting in the United States—he claimed one evening to have counted 184 UFOs passing over Palomar Gardens." She stopped reading to look up at me. "It's nice that he thought to count them, don't you think?"

"I do. So he was an early-day ufologist."

"Early-day crackpot is more like it."

"So what else?"

"So not long after that he's writing books, giving lectures, making a bit of money . . ."

"When?"

"When he meets an alien. This was out in the desert. His name was Orthon, from Venus. This was in 1952."

"Venus? So no Martians or Lunarians?"

"Apparently not," she said, laughing as she put her hand on my arm. "What they say is that on November 20, 1952, Adamski and several friends were in the Colorado Desert near the town of Desert Center, California, when they purportedly saw a large submarine-shaped object hovering in the sky. Believing that the ship was looking for him, Adamski is said to have left his friends and to have headed away from the main road. Shortly afterwards, according to Adamski's accounts, a scout ship made of a type of translucent metal landed close to him, and its pilot, a Venusian called Orthon, disembarked and sought him out. Adamski claimed that the people with him also saw the Venusian ship, and several of them later stated they could see Adamski meeting someone in the desert, although from a considerable distance." She looked up at me. "Why does stuff like this always happen out in the desert?"

"No."

"No what?"

"No, we're not driving out to Desert Center, wherever that is."

"You don't think Orthon is still dropping by, do you? But he does sound interesting. Long blond hair, humanoid, telepathic, love, wisdom . . . I guess he warned Adamski about nuclear war."

"Today he'd warn him about climate change. What else?"

"Oh, just some more craziness. Like how in 1953 he and this Irish guy wrote a book, *Flying Saucers Have Landed*, which apparently sold quite well."

"So a bit of fame *and* fortune."

"Also that this Irish guy made a low-budget UFO film, *Them And The Thing*, at his home, Castle Leslie."

"His home was a castle?"

"So they say. *Desmond Leslie, aristocratic Irish eccentric.* Then in 1955, another book, *Inside the Space Ships*, which is his account of a trip he took with Orthon—"

"To Venus?"

"All over. And this is cool. He said that on another trip he met the Master, this thousand year old guy who was the elder philosopher of the space people."

"The Master?"

"That's what it says. That Adamski was told he'd been selected by these Nordic aliens to bring their message of peace to Earth people. That throughout history other humans had also served as their messengers. Jesus Christ, for example. That even now these aliens were peacefully living on Earth. Adamski said he'd even met with some of them in bars and restaurants in Southern California."

"Also right here in this campground would be my guess. Maybe even tonight."

"I'd rather not."

"Any more?"

"Lots, but that's the gist of it, other than how he was dating a couple of them, Kalna and Illmuth."

"Aliens?"

"Uh-huh. Blondes."

"You bought his books, didn't you?" That was her question for me the next morning when I got back from the little convenience store.

"I did. I also had an interesting chat with the kid working over there. According to him, they're still seeing UFOs around here."

"You didn't happen to ask him about Orthon, did you?"

"I started to, but then I got this strange feeling like he might be one of them. You know, one of those Venusians who walk amongst us."

"Did he have blond hair?"

"Actually, he did. Sort of tall, too."

"Wow. I hope you can use that in your book."

"I don't see how."

5

HOW'S IT GOING?

So, you ask, how was that first night in an RV? Pretty nice, actually, they're much more comfortable than I'd anticipated. We slid the dinette out, which made for a cozy little nook, I prepared a tasty dinner, it was sort of like sleeping in our own little apartment out among the oaks.

But now I'm wondering if this might not also be good time to say something about sex. It's true, I have been putting it off, but only because it's such a generic topic. It's not like we aren't all familiar with it. So let me just say that with Cyd it was never anything but recreational. She'd had sex with so many different men it just wasn't possible for it to be anything else, or so I've always believed. So that special significance it frequently has for the rest of us just wasn't there. "Wow, really working away down there, aren't you?" is what she said, but said with a lot of humor as she patted my back. And I really was, all *Sturm und Drang*, just laboring away, best effort and all that. "You mean this is supposed to be fun?" And of course that got a big laugh because that was just her point. So we reached an understanding right away, and after that we had fun a lot.

And that place where she was staying over in Brentwood? On Bristol? That was the guesthouse of a well-know producer, if a 3,500 square foot house can be called a guesthouse; if staying there for over a year can be called being a guest. No, nothing sexual, she was a very close friend of his wife, a woman she'd known for years since they'd both been teenagers starring in one of those dreadful mixed-family sitcoms of the 1990s. She, Lisa, was a lovely woman, and always very sympathetic whenever we talked about Cyd. I know she was hoping I'd be moving in, but of course that never happened.

She loved Julian, and we had to stop so she could check out the craft stores, buy an apple pie, which was delicious, and marvel at how close we still were to the coast. Then it was off to the desert, down Banner Grade past the tourmaline mines I knew of and on to Calexico, though we actually spent that night in El Centro. But what about Calexico? Well, we were tired and there was El Centro, and frankly it's a much nicer place to stay. As for getting around, it didn't really make that much difference. We'd already talked about it, how we were limited by where we could drive our Minnie Winnie. I know, we should have done what other RVers do, towed a small car, kept a motorbike handy, put a bicycle or two in that rack on the back, but we'd done none of that.

"Does Dion stay in El Centro?"

"He does now."

"So it *was* a good idea to drive down here and see for ourselves?"

"Yes, thank you, not that it's going to matter to any of my readers. Like how you seem to think they'll all be flocking here next winter."

"But you know what, that's not such a bad idea. Next winter, why don't you travel around in an RV, hit all the big RV parks, promote your books, get a film crew to come out and follow you around, then sell it to one of those travel channels." She stopped to look at me. "No?"

"No, and not because it's not a good idea. It really would make for some good reality TV. But because there's very little overlap between my readers and RVers."

"Are you sure?"

"I've never seen any evidence of it."

"So we've got an untapped market. Nothing wrong with that, especially now that your books are going to be so much more authentic." Yes, she was laughing.

6

THE IMPERIAL VALLEY

El Centro is very flat. Did you know you're actually below sea level out there in the Imperial Valley? It certainly feels like it. The air is thick, warm, balmy, soft on the skin, and there's this smell in the air, moisture in the desert, growing things, a salty-dusty note I like. It's the same in Calexico, which is only two or three miles to the south right snug up against the border. So now I was thinking Dion would be surprised by Mexicali's size; that maybe the Gustafsons liked getting over there and he began tagging along. It is the Imperial Valley's largest city, with close to 700,000 people versus Calexico's 40,000 and El Centro's 45,000. Why so big? Maybe it's all the maquiladoras. Hey, how's that for verisimilitude? Because she just kept stuffing my head with facts. Making sure I was cognizant of the *big picture*. Yes, but what about all those more fine-grained details my readers like? Well, those would just have wait, springing as they almost always do mostly from my imagination. I was also starting to get this bad feeling about the Gustafsons, like maybe they'd get in a jam over on the other side of the border and Dion would have to do his thing. If so, Cyd was going to be very upset. So I tried this out on her.

"Dion, is that guy dead?" He was walking with Don past an alleyway in Mexicali, over there looking for cheap Lipitor and something nice for Donna.

"The way he's slumped over like that, sure looks like it. Come on," he said, taking Don's arm, "we need to get out of here."

"But—"

"If we stay we're going to have to answer a lot of questions. Then we'll probably be here all day."

"So we just leave him?"

"Everyone else has."

"What do you think?"

"I think it's very unlikely. We certainly didn't see anything like that over there today. Why should they?" We'd driven the Minnie Winnie down to the border, then parked and walked across. Pretty much a waste of time since there wasn't much to see up that close to the border. We should have hopped on a bus and gone downtown instead.

"So what would you have them see? And remember, it's got to be something that presents them with a mystery, or at least with a dangerous situation."

"I have no idea, but I'd hardly call walking around dangerous."

"Okay, so what about this? They're over there walking around. Right? Then they see this wallet lying in the street, but just as they're about to pick it up the police arrive."

"Mexican police? That's such a cliché. Better if there's someone following them."

"The killer?"

"You know, it would really help if you had some idea where this was headed."

"Yes, but think how boring that would be to write."

"So why not do something with that article you read this morning? About that woman who worked in an insurance office and did all that money laundering for the drug cartels."

"All right. So how does that work? How do we hook her up with Dion?"

"He sleeps with her?" Well, at that I just had to laugh because that's probably how I would write it, even though it's not very plausible. Come on, this is Dion we're talking about, I'm not so sure he even likes women. "But then you rarely have him with a woman," she said. "I've been wondering about that."

"And you're asking me? Blame the women. Like you, would you find him attractive?"

"No, but I still might still feel sorry for him. He is kind of pathetic." And of course I had to think about that remark for the rest of the day, wondering if that was how she really felt about me. It was entirely possible.

"It was nothing, probably just a raccoon." This was around three in the morning after she'd heard a noise. She thought someone was trying the door. I didn't say it, but that seemed highly unlikely given that we were parked in the middle of a dozen or so RVs.

"Do they have raccoons in the desert?"

"Yes."

"But you don't really know, do you?" she said, rolling over on her side.

"No."

"Except in your books."

"Have I had a raccoon in one of my books?"

"You know, Dion would get his gun and go see."

"Yes, I'm sure he would, but I don't have a gun." She was staring at me with that look people get while they wait for you to finally get to it. "Fine, I'll take a look, but if it bites me and I get rabies . . ."

It was pretty dark, with just a couple of security lights down at the end of our row, but then that's the desert at night, surprisingly dark. So that's why I stood there waiting for my eyes to adjust, listening to the distant hiss of trucks and cars out on the highway. It was just so quiet, like one of those age restricted suburban neighborhoods. That's when I finally noticed that the storage bins along the bottom of our Minnie were open. Okay, that's no raccoon, that's the first thing I thought, also how much I wished Dion really were there, but mostly I was thinking that I'd do just about anything to keep them away from Cyd.

"You know," I said, speaking into the darkness, "I've already called 911." That's when I heard them, or at least their feet scuffling in the gravel behind me. No, of course I didn't want to turn around, but you know, sometimes you just do. Shadows. Moving shadows, then a young man coming at me swinging something. Crowbar. Then the RV's exterior lights came on and I heard her say, "Frosty?" Startled, he turned to see, that's when I grabbed his arm, then kneed him in the groin. "Give me that," I said, wrenching the crowbar away from him. "You're not going to hit him are you?" she said. "Stay inside," I told her. Then he was moaning, gasping for breath as he tried to stand. "You little fucker," I said.

"Tell your friends to clear out or I'm going to beat the shit out you with this thing."

"Whoa, man," he said, holding up his hands as I raised the crowbar like I meant to conk him.

"Frosty!"

"Jesus, will you just stay inside."

"But he's just a kid."

Was he? Well, yeah, surprisingly he was. I hadn't noticed. "Some kid," I said. "He might have killed me with this thing."

"Maybe he's just scared."

"Yeah, and maybe I'd just be dead."

So the way this played out in real life, she first calmed me down, then talked the kid into being still so she could ask if I'd hurt him. As she did I walked over to the two lawn chairs they'd pulled from one of the storage bins, picked one up, unfolded it, and sat down to watch. You know, he really did look sort of pathetic, so leaning over I grabbed the other chair and handed it to him. "Here you go, you little fucker," I said. Still wary, he nevertheless took it, though by now he was obviously much more interested in Cyd. Well, what male past puberty wouldn't be, especially in that long t-shirt she wore—nothing like a beautiful woman to settle you down in a more watchful frame of mind. Then she was standing there frowning at us, hands on her hips, the perfect picture of the matriarch.

"You might have killed him," she said to me. "And you, this is what you do, sneak around at night stealing things?"

At a loss for words, he turned to look at me. "Hey," I said, "you're on your own."

"What's your name?" she asked.

"Lonnie."

"Lonnie what?"

Again, he looked at me, so I said to her, "Don't ask him that, he thinks you'll tell the cops. Right?"

He nodded.

"Cops? I was going to call his mother."

"Well, Lonnie, now you've done it, put us both at the mercy of the ladies." Then to her: "You don't suppose the prisoners could have a beer?" I looked at him. "Dude?" That's when he smiled.

Anyway, she did call his mother and his brother came by the park to pick him up. One of those tattooed gang-banger types, and I thought, well, if it had been you, bro, I would have conked you, but Lonnie got in the car and off they went.

"Looks like the beautiful lady just saved another life," I said when I returned.

"He really was just a kid, Frosty."

"Yeah, well you should have seen big brother. I sure hope he doesn't decide to come by for a beer."

"Are you really worried?"

"No, but it's probably time for us to pull up stakes anyway. You know, off in search of more authentic experiences for my book."

"That will do."

"Just teasing. But you do have to admit it's quite a shock when real life suddenly erupts like that right in the middle of your novel."

"Speaking of which . . ."

"Add Lonnie to my story?"

"Well, you have been wondering how to get Dion together with the lady doing the money laundering."

"If that's what I decide to do."

"Haven't you?"

I suppose I had, and she was right, it was perfect. Dion calls the kid's mother up, she comes over to get him, all apologetic, angry at her son, telling Dion about how hard it is to raise a kid without a father, that sort of thing, and then, soon, she's sleeping with him, he gets a feel for the kid, a grudging bond develops, all stupidly melodramatic, of course, and then she levels with him— she's got a problem. So I wrote this:

"Don, are you okay?"

"He's fine, Donna." He helped him up. "So, what do you think? Call the cops, or beat the crap out of him?"

"I know what I'd like to do," he said.

"Me too, but he really is just a kid. My guess, we'd be in a lot more trouble than he is." He knew he was right. Plus, there'd be some sort of activist around who'd be tight with the local authorities, and here they were, outsiders, Anglos, beating up this poor kid. He's just poor; they're racists. That's how the game is played.

"Then call his mother," Donna said.

He looked at Don and smiled. Actually, they both smiled. Of course she'd say that, like all it took was a mom. If only. But there was certainly no point in calling the cops. It really would be nothing but a big hassle for them if they did. Then they'd drag them all back down there to testify or give depositions. No, it would just be a big waste of time.

He looked at the kid, still sitting there in the lawn chair. "What's your name?"

"Why should I tell you?"

"Because if you don't we'll get your damn wallet and see for ourselves."

"Juan."

"Okay, Juan, here's what we'll do. Juan?" He kicked one of the legs of the chair so he'd look at him.

"What?"

"Nice and polite now, tell the lady your momma's phone number."

So that's how he met Estella Torres-Martinez.

"Well?"

"I like it," she said. Then she grinned. "See? Never would've happened if we hadn't been down here."

We'd hit the road early, escaping the consequences of our good deed, or at least that's how I viewed it, and now we were parked behind Johnny's Burritos in Brawley just back from our early lunch—machaca with egg breakfast burrito for me, carne asada torta for her—while I sat in my captain's chair typing away.

"You know, I'm tempted to put Johnny's in my book."

"I thought you didn't do travelogue?" she teased.

"Oh? So now you don't think it's worth it?" I knew she did. She'd spent fifteen minutes on the web reading restaurant reviews for Brawley. Johnny's was her choice.

"So I guess that means Dion's going to Brawley."

"He might. We've got to get him up to Slab City somehow."

"And Estella?"

"I'm pretty sure she goes along. She should, shouldn't she?"

"How should I know? You haven't written that part yet."

No, she was going. Why else would they end up in Slab City? On the run . . . because of her . . . it didn't make any sense if she wasn't there. "So how does this sound? The cartel has these hit men after her. Then the whole thing gets dropped in Dion's lap. So they bug out. End up in Slab City."

"But why Slab City?"

"Because that's the title of my book."

"And that's it? Just because that's what you came up with for a title?"

"Hey, inspiration can come from anywhere, all that matters is what you do with it."

"Writers!" she said, shaking her head.

"Why do you always say that? Like we're this lower form of life." I raised my eyebrows a bit to stare at her. "Sounds like there might be something personal in this."

"Bastard wrote me out of the show. Lied about it, of course. Then we get the script for the last episode of the season and I'm dying in the hospital."

"From what?"

"Boyfriend beats me up, which was just what he wanted to do."

"He was your boyfriend?"

"At one time, but I'd moved on—"

"You do that, don't you? Just move on."

"Sometimes," she said with a shrug.

"So being a writer, and I assume this is your point, he took his revenge where he could, in the realm of imagination."

"He wrote me out of the show, Frosty. That wasn't in anyone's imagination."

"No, I understand that, I just meant that being a writer he was free to do imaginatively what he wasn't free to do in fact. Beat you up, I mean." Then I laughed. "But that's probably because he knew you'd whip his ass." She was very fit. Women in her business, women in their late thirties, well, they stayed in shape.

"It wouldn't have been hard. Most of you guys are real pussies."

"Not me. I really smacked that kid around last night, remember?"

"I do. What a tough guy."

7

184 FEET BELOW SEA LEVEL

"Listen to some of these names." She was referring to the names of some of the nearby towns in the Imperial Valley. "Citrus View, Hovley, Munyon, Orita, Fondo, Verdant, Calipatria, Niland—"

"Niland?"

"From *Nile Land*. Mundo, Iris, Tortuga, Wister, Frink, Bombay Beach, Durmid, Ferrum, Mortmar . . . well, they just go on and on. Mecca, Valerie, Plaster City. Really, you couldn't make these up if you tried. And this is interesting: at an elevation of 180 feet below sea level, Calipatria has the lowest elevation of any city in the western hemisphere. At 184 feet, the city currently claims to have the tallest flagpole, ensuring that the American flag always flies above sea level, although according to the Guinness Book of World Records the world's tallest flagpole is the Jeddah Flagpole, but that's entirely above sea level." She paused to look out the windshield. "I'd like to see that," she said.

"You will, we're headed straight for it, and thanks for the travel tips. I'm sure my readers will be very pleased."

"Only if you use them in your book, which I very much doubt."

"Don't be so sure, I'm beginning to think Dion needs to be more cognizant of his surroundings."

"Only because you suddenly are."

"Pull up over there," Estella said, pointing to a gravel road out to one of the head gates on the canal. "See if you can get us behind that mesquite." He turned off a little ways up the road, then carefully drove across the barren field to a shallow depression behind a stand of honey mesquite.

"Not easy to hide one of these things," he said.

"No, but it's almost dark, they'll never see us over here if we're careful."

"And tomorrow?"

"I'm not sure. What do you think?"

"I think we should hole up with that live-free-or-die crowd over in Slab City for a few days."

"Not make a run for I-10?"

"Only because that's just what they'll be expecting us to do. Desperate, on the run, trying to get to Palm Springs or L.A. before it's too late." Then nodding at the RV, "And we won't be very hard to spot."

The whole thing had quickly gone off the rails, but then there's never any arguing with guys like Grijalva. He'd told him she didn't take any of his money, that so far she'd given the Feds nothing, but none of that really solved Grijalva's problem. He could see it, he was overwhelmed, trying to keep too many balls in the air at the same time. In those circumstances the easiest thing, the quickest thing, was to simplify. It was clear what that meant. Gregson? No, so far the Feds had been useless. Frankly, he wasn't so sure they weren't compromised. That was a lot of money floating around out there. It looked to him like someone got tempted. How else was Grijalva so well informed?

"Dion?"

He looked at her and smiled. "Sorry, just trying to fit together a few more pieces of our little puzzle."

"You're not still mad at me, are you?"

"No. You were right, there was no need." At least not then, as for the future, well, he still might need to deal with Grijalva in a more definitive fashion.

"Uh, haven't we skipped a few things?"

"Sorry, that's just how I like to write. Sustain that momentum. Come back later to flesh things out."

"And who's this Grijalva?"

"He's the bad guy."

"That you just made up. And really, Frosty, in a more *definitive* fashion?"

"I know," I said, laughing with her. "But when you write this kind of stuff you come to rely on your euphemisms."

"Can't just say kill?"

"Can, and do, but after a while that gets tiresome for my readers. It's the same in your line of work. Otherwise, it's just too obvious how this is just a little more of that same old same old."

"I see. So it won't be long before it's time for Dion to go back and settle things definitively."

"Don't you want him to? Isn't that one of the pleasures of my books, when Dion finally reaches that point of no return? When he's forced to become a man of action? Finally freed from self-doubt and the pangs of a guilty conscience to once again set the natural order to right."

"That's your definition of justice?"

"It's Dion's. And what is justice? Isn't it basically just reestablishing some sort of harmony in the world?"

"But only if it's done definitively."

"I'd expect no less of him."

"But their immediate problem was how to disappear for a few weeks. He was sure that's all it would take. The situation was far too volatile to remain as it was. Of course there was no going back for Estella—ever. She knew that. Her old life was gone. As for a new one, well, he'd do what he could, but that wasn't going to be much. He'd get her to safety, make sure she really was, but that would be that. Maybe she'd blend in up in Orange County where Juan was, keeping out of sight with the Gustafson's in that RV park in Hermosa Beach.

"They are finally safe, aren't they?"
"Still worrying about the Gustafsons?"
"Can you blame me? I keep expecting to read how you've killed them off and poor Juan is on the run."
"You know, that's not a bad idea."
"Frosty . . ."
"No, they're fine, and who knows, I may need them again in another book."

But is that what he really wanted? To just walk away like that? He'd never really thought about it before, what it would be like with Estella. But that was crazy. It came down to trust. He'd never be able to trust her; trust that she'd been honest with him at any point. Not that he could blame her. She'd found herself in a desperate situation, then she'd found a way out. Him. They'd never get around that. So he was just going to set that all aside. Better that way. He had his life, he'd just get on with it.

"Too bad," she said.

"Not really. Guy's a loner. That's the only way it works. We get to see how it tempts him, but then we also see how foolish it would be for him to try."

"So who's he going to kill? Because it seems like we're just about ready for some action."

"I want to get them up to Slab City, first. Then they need to hide out with those snowbirds and that live-free-or-die crowd for a few days, which will give me an opportunity to work in some of those gritty details you've been feeding me. Then we kill people."

"What about us? Slab City for two?"

"Got to. You've got me totally hooked on this realism thing."

8

IT AIN'T NO TOWN AND IT AIN'T NO CITY

"It was originally called Camp Dunlap. Marines. 1942."

"For?"

"Artillery." Again, she was reading to me. Offering up a running commentary on where we were. "But they shut that down in 1956, then came in and hauled everything away except for the concrete slabs."

"Hence *Slab City*."

"Yes, but that had to wait until 1965."

"Seriously? 1965? Because there's this guy who's written a book about that, how everything seems to happen in 1965."

"What book?"

"*1965.* So what did happen?"

"According to Wikipedia this all began with some snowbirds who were staying up north in a place called Painted Canyon."

"Up north?"

"Up in the hills somewhere out east of Mecca. I know," she said, grinning at me, "it really is just too perfect. But it sounds like they'd built themselves this shantytown all hidden away up there just minding their own business, so naturally the state had to come in and run them off."

"Naturally. Then they migrated down here."

"Some of them did."

"It sounds biblical. Cast out, the exiles wandered in the barren wilderness until they came upon the slabs. Or maybe it's more like Brigham Young: *This is the place.*"

"Yes, this place. The last free place in America."

"Exactly. And why is that so difficult; finding a place where you'll be left alone?"

"But isn't that what Dion's doing, one RV park at a time?"

"Well, in some sense I suppose he is. Not that we all aren't, each in our own way. But I'd hate to think our quest necessarily leads us here, to Slab City."

"But now Dion *is* here."

"I know. Which means it's time for him to get tangled up with those cartel shooters."

"You mean it's time for mayhem."

"Past time, though I'm still not sure how this is supposed to play out."

"What about a car bomb? Like what they did to me in this soap opera I was in. No, not another boyfriend," she said, smiling at me. "I just wanted more money."

"Too dramatic, especially since they're supposed to be hiding out. And since Dion's an ex-cop . . ."

"Has to be a gun?"

"Has to be a gun."

They slept well that night, then in the morning drove on in to Slab City, not that it was much of a city, not in any ordinary sense, though you definitely felt you were somewhere, somewhere with at least some notion of being a place. RVs, campers, trailers, tents, old buses, every sort of makeshift shelter one might imagine, but all dusty and gritty, with trash and junk lying around everywhere, all very post-apocalypse. But then your eyes got used to it and you started to see there was order, though very much homegrown and organic; that things weren't nearly as tenuous as they at first appeared to be.

"Well," Dion said, "I'm amazed. Have you ever been up here before?"

"Never," Estella said. "It's not exactly my sort of place, you know?"

"All Anglos, or not middle-class?"

"Both, or so I've always assumed." She was looking at some of the big RVs, thinking those weren't cheap.

"Aren't you going to mention Salvation Mountain? They must have driven right past it on their way in. We did."

"Do you really think I should? I don't want to get bogged down in a lot of boring detail. Yes, I know, *but your readers love that sort of thing.*"

"They do."

"I don't see why. It's just some crazy old desert rat who got it in his head to build his own mountain and then cover it over with bible verses."

"It's still pretty amazing."

"What's amazing is what too much sun and heat can do."

"Make you crazy?"

"Monotheism."

"Let's stop up there and see about finding a place to settle in."

"You think it really matters? These people are all over the place." It mattered. He could see that, how even here there were boundaries, some faint echo of what it meant to possess private property. *This little patch of desert may not legally be mine, but you'd better believe it's mine while I'm here.* Fine, all they wanted to do was blend in and be invisible for a few days.

They pulled up next to a ramshackle collection of shacks, trailers, and cars, most of which were covered by a large tent-like tarp. "You'd better wait here," he told her.

At first he didn't see anyone, but it was dark and it took a moment for his eyes to adjust, then he saw a man and woman sitting at a card table working on what he took to be a large cardboard sign. "Sorry, don't mean to interrupt," he said when the man looked up. "But this place sort of has the look of something official, and, well, we've got a few questions, if you don't mind."

"Not at all, that's why we're here, in an unofficial capacity only, of course."

"Yep. Unofficial, that's the word for us," the woman added. "I'm Marie, by the way, he's Tim. What can we do for you?"

"Well, I suppose all we really need is a place to park our RV, but I wasn't sure what the protocol was. Looks like everyone's already got their spot all staked out. Just didn't want to upset anyone."

"Problem is, you're late," the man said. "All the good spots are taken. But that's okay, you just follow any of our lovely streets far enough and you'll eventually find plenty of vacancies."

"It's a big desert," she said. "Always room for more."

"I was wondering. You know, this place gets a lot of press—that's why we're here—but we were worried, maybe it's all filled up."

"It's certainly a lot more crowded around here than it used to be, that's for sure, but we don't mind, might help keep the politicians from selling it out from under our feet."

"Is that what they're up to?"

"Well, look around, does this look like the sort of place they can tolerate?"

"Yeah, I was wondering about that. There used to be this place up near Phoenix, Camp Eagle, then the BLM came sneaking in one night and ran everyone off."

"Know all about that," Tim said. "Bunch of destitute economic refugees. Where were they supposed to go?"

"Internment camps," Marie said. "Just a matter of time."

"Jesus, is that really possible? All we want to do is get away from winter for a few months."

"Where're you from?" Tim asked.

"Back East. Philly. Wife and I, we're finally taking that Western vacation we've been talking about ever since we retired. Got a son up in San Francisco. Sort of headed his way, but taking it nice and slow."

"Tim, tell 'em about the tanks."

"Tanks? You mean like Patton's?"

Laughing, Tim said, "He was around here, for sure, but these are just some empty water tanks about a half mile up the road. She means that's a nice spot. Most people don't get up there. But you get out there and it's real nice. Sort of a mesquite bosque where there used to be a spring. I guess it's still there . . ."

"It's there, but it's not much, not anymore," she said. "But it still makes for a nice, pretty little spot."

"I can't believe how you just make this stuff up."

"But we did see a place like that. You even said it was some sort of unofficial town hall, or at least where people went to gossip and leave messages."

"And the tanks?"

"Well," and I laughed, because that's just what you do, writing shit like this, you improvise. "The Marines probably had water tanks around here somewhere, and there's the Coachella Canal, so I was thinking, well, okay, so at one time there was this spring, and it's still wet enough out there to support this picturesque little mesquite grove."

"So Dion and Estella get out there and do what, wait for the shooters? Because I don't see how they're going to find them if that's where they pitch camp."

"Maybe Dion finds them."

"Okay," she said, slowly nodding her head. "That works. But maybe he sees Tim first. Then Tim tells him there were these newcomers asking questions. Made him suspicious. So he tells Dion—"

"Which is when Dion goes hunting for them. I like it. It's always better for my readers, anyway, when Dion assumes the role of the aggressor."

"Goes bad-ass."

"But only in small doses. We can't let him go completely rogue."

"Because he's still an ex-cop."

"Exactly."

9

THE FOUNTAIN OF YOUTH

But we didn't stay in Slab City, for the most part it really does look like a dump and neither of us felt comfortable around all those eccentrics and people of questionable intent. Yes, there were a few legitimate snowbirds and some fancy rigs, but mostly they were off by themselves keeping their distance from the less well-organized types. And then most of the good spots really were taken, but not up at The Fountain of Youth Spa Resort, which is roughly ten miles north of Slab City along the Coachella Canal. Cyd found it reading their rave reviews in Yelp. It was a good choice, and who knows, maybe I'll be back someday when I'm a little older to spend a pleasant winter hanging out with my new seniors pals. It's quite a contrast, how these elderly snowbirds go about organizing themselves, their social activities and so on, versus that Wild West style down in Slab City.

I was pleased, not only did we have our pick of several nice spots, no one seemed to mind that it would be for just one night. Cyd had mentioned a swim, so once we were settled that's the first thing we did, followed by a leisurely stroll around the resort as we dried off. Up and down the long rows of RVs and campers, the place immaculate, everyone very friendly and curious about who we were, but as you might expect it really was lights out by 10 p.m.

Back in our Minnie, she said, "Other than not costing anything, I really don't see what other advantages there are to staying down in Slab City. Yeah, some of that art stuff was interesting, but that's about it."

"Not that legendary, iconoclastic rebel vibe? All that business about doing whatever you want, whenever you want to do it?"

"But that's a myth. You saw all those rules at East Jesus." There was a long list of dos and don'ts, which, if studied long enough, painted a rather vivid portrait of what life there was really like.

"But you need to consider who most of those people are. Hardly takes a sociologist to predict there'd be petty crime, irresponsible behavior, and a distinct lack of community. *Just leave me alone* isn't much of a foundation to build upon."

"And here?"

"Nice middle-class retirees who've spent a lifetime getting their shit together. Community just comes naturally to them."

"Hollywood's got it all wrong, haven't they, all that *Mad Max* stuff?"

"You mean it's these old gray heads who'll be the survivors?"

"Won't they? They'll still be out here playing bingo and bocci ball, having barbeques and dances, while everyone down in Slab City is killing each other or starving to death."

"Which is why we've got Dion down there and not up here, although this would be a much better place for him to hide out. Just blend in with the seniors. Who'd know?"

"Yes, but given your penchant for killing off snowbirds, sooner or later there'd be all sorts of distressing collateral damage."

"True, but there's always my next book."

"Frosty, really, I'm begging you, okay? Just let them be." But then she grinned at me. "Though if you were to write it . . ."

What would I call it? Well, I don't know, what would you suggest?"

"*Drowning in the Fountain of Youth*?"

"Oh, excellent."

The next morning they were having a special pancake breakfast we made sure to attend. It was a fundraiser of some sort for the local chapter of the Rotary Club, not exactly sure for what, but the pancakes were good and so was the company. Afterwards, we hit the pool again, then came back and relaxed in the RV.

"So that Mrs. Martin sure likes you."

"Susie?"

"Oh?" she grinned. "So now it's Susie."

"There's just something about Canadian women in their seventies." She and her husband, Tony, were from Moose Jaw.

"I still wonder if we're not making a mistake, not bringing Dion up here."

"No. Too genteel." Frankly, knowing Dion, I just couldn't see him fitting in. First of all, not old enough, second, too much of a loner, and then all those planned activities would drive him crazy. But maybe I'm wrong. Maybe even a fictional character can change.

"Too bad. I was thinking it might be nice to give your readers someplace pleasant to stay."

"Slab City isn't that bad, just have to bring your own RV. But then they'd expect that."

"Yes, your ideal reader. Someone who not only can afford an RV, but feels compelled to retrace your footsteps."

"I know. Sort of like the Camino de Santiago in Spain. A sacred pilgrimage."

"St. Dion?" She shook her head. "Not in my church. By the way, did you tell Susie about your books?"

"No. I told her I was a retired cop and you were this parolee I'd helped go straight."

"Parolee?"

"That's what I told her."

"What did she say?"

"She wondered if you'd been a hooker."

"I have played a hooker."

"She thinks you could make a lot of money around here."

"You didn't really say that."

"I certainly didn't tell her I wrote RV park murder mysteries."

There came a point in mid-morning when we had to decide whether to stay for another night or push on for Palm Springs. We were definitely tempted, no question about it—it really is that nice—but that would have meant paying for an extra day and night in the Minnie.

"So?" she asked when I came back from the office.

"Just like you said, they were very sorry to see us go. *You sure you don't want to spend another night?*"

"We're not sure!"

"Yeah, and what makes this even worse, I'm standing there chatting when one of them mentions that the radio-controlled airplane club is having their meeting this afternoon."

"I don't know, all those old duffers out there, planes zooming around."

"Yeah, but I bet Dion would like it. If he ever gets up here."

10

WHAT'S IN A NAME

We had this crazy conversation on the way over to Palm Springs.

"Do you know what Esposito means?" She was looking at her iPhone.

"Dion's Esposito? I know what it means for me, the hockey player, Phil Esposito." But why I'd picked that name I have no idea. I've never followed hockey, and Esposito was way before my time.

"But the name itself, what that means?"

"Googling, are we?"

"It's from the Latin, *expositus*, which means exposed."

"Okay."

"So the surname, Esposito, that's what they gave to foundlings."

"Foundlings? All of them? That's just so bizarre."

"Any abandoned kid left at a church or monastery, that's the name they got."

"Incredible. But then that's Dion, isn't it? Even his family tree's a dead end. So what about Dion?"

"You've never done this?"

"Checked out his name? No, why should I?"

"So you just picked Dion because . . .?"

"Well, I didn't exactly just pick it . . ." and I hesitated, but then it's just a silly name.

"Yes?"

"It's from Dion and the Belmonts. Ever hear of them? *Runaround Sue*? *The Wanderer*?" She shook her head. "So they're from Philly, Dion's from Philly, it just came to me. Why? You think these names have some special significance? They're just names. Go ahead, Google Dion and the Belmonts. You'll see."

"Just a moment," she said. "Ah. Here we go, Dion and the Belmonts. And there's Mr. DiMucci. Oops."

"Oops what?"

"You said Philly, right? Because they're from the Bronx."

"No way. All those do-wop groups were from Philly."

"Not these guys," and she held her iPhone out for me to see. "Wow, poor Dion, not only does he have an orphan's name, you didn't even have the right city."

"So what about Dion?"

"What's it mean?"

"Yeah. See what it says."

"Well," she said, looking at her iPhone. "I guess it's from Dionysus, so that's not so bad, being named after a Greek god."

Not being the beneficiary of a classical education, I knew next to nothing about any of this. But now I've read up on it. So there he was, Dionysus, just another abandoned child, though in this case sown into his father's thigh (Zeus) for safekeeping. And then there's all that business about wine making, Dionysian frenzy, ecstasy, and intoxication, which is certainly intriguing but hardly characterizes my Dion who's usually sober and rarely given to frenzy of any sort. Far more Apollonian than Dionysian is what Nietzsche would say, but when you're stuck with an ill-considered name, fictional or otherwise, well, that's just the way it goes.

So we'd cleared the Imperial Valley for the Coachella, well on our way up to Palm Springs finally free of Cyd's incessant hunt for authenticity. I wasn't surprised, by the way, that she'd never heard of Dion and the Belmonts. She is younger than me (she was born in 1979), not that I'm all that old, but I like a lot of that older stuff and apparently she doesn't. But them came a troubling admission as we neared Indio.

"Did you go to Desert Trip?"

"What?"

"Music festival. I was just wondering, since it was right along here."

Turns out, she and a bunch of her friends had flown out with some producer pal for this music festival in Indio featuring all these antique rock stars: Dylan, The Rolling Stones, The Who, Neil Young, Paul McCartney. Then they'd flown out the following weekend for more, staying at this guy's spread over in Rancho Mirage. So I told her, no, I'd never even heard of it. Also that I was a bit surprised to hear she'd been that interested. To which she replied, "Something to do?" shrugging her shoulders like that might be a problem for her, needing something to do.

"So how was it?"

"The music was fine, if you like that sort of thing, but the event was great. Huge crowds. The buzz about who was there."

"In the crowd? The celebrities?"

"That's right."

"This is the same place where they have that big music festival every year?" She nodded. "Interesting. It must have been nice to see Dylan."

"I suppose. I've never been that big a fan."

"Because you're not old enough, like with Dion and the Belmonts. Dylan probably even knows Dion." Did he really? Seems unlikely, but she wouldn't know that. "So aside from the music, you still had a good time."

"You sound disapproving."

"Do I? I don't mean to."

"You sure?"

"Of course. I get why these festivals are popular. How people need to share in something that gives their lives meaning and purpose. It only bothers me when it gets too tribal; all that us versus them stuff. But even then it's usually harmless."

"Though not always."

"No."

Then she began to connect the dots. "So Dion, he doesn't really have a tribe, does he? But then neither do you. Not that you're as big a loner, but then you're hardly the sort to stand in line waiting to join something."

"Depends on what I'm joining."

"No it doesn't."

"And you? I'd hardly call how you've lived your life normal."

"No."

"And I'm not that disapproving. I've been to festivals. Burning Man, for instance."

"Really? Because Lisa and I have been talking about that for years." This was Lisa, her charming landlady in Brentwood.

"You probably didn't notice, but did you read what it said about Burning Man in our rental agreement? It was very explicit, *no Burning Man*, which makes a lot of sense since it's just out there in the desert and they're all stoners."

"So if Lisa and I went, would you come?"

"Buy me a Minnie and I will."

"Frosty! Did you hear what you just said? You're beginning to sound like a real RVer."

"Which should make you and Dion very happy."

"*Burnt to a Crisp at Burning Man?*" she said, grinning at me.

"If I wrote it, you mean?"

"If you did."

"But it's still going to need a geographical reference, like my other books. *Black Rock City Bonfire*, for example"

"Because it's in Black Rock City?"

"Uh-huh."

"But then how do we get Dion up there?" I have to say, Cyd was very helpful, very clever, really a wonderful pal. My guess, everyone felt that way about her. But that's a double-edged sword, isn't it? Since we rarely settle down with a pal for more than a few happy days.

"Oh," I said, smiling at her. "I'm sure you'll come up with something."

"I'm curious. When you went, where did you stay?"

"I drove my father up and we slept in my car. This was back in the '90s when everything was still free. It's a much bigger deal now."

"You took your father to Burning Man?"

"More like he took me. He's . . . well, let's just say he's a character. It was sort of my thirtieth birthday present. He thought I'd like it, and it's not like that New Age stuff is unknown in our family."

"What New Age stuff?"

"Gestalt therapist at Esalen. My mother's counseling practice."

"Counseling for what?"

"You really don't know anything about this stuff, do you?" If she had she would have known it was almost always for something sexual."

"I know Esalen is down in Big Sur."

"Yes, but we lived in Carmel Valley. Actually, my parents still do." Just up the road from Joan Baez is how they liked to describe it. Just another bit of generational lore—their generation—that meant nothing to me.

"And yet they named you Frosty."

"Only because they like to tease. It's never bothered me."

"Weren't you teased at school?"

"Not as a kid, but I didn't go to public schools until I was fourteen. Then you just smack a few kids in the nose and that's the end of it."

"Frosty, I'm amazed. I had no idea you came from such an interesting family."

"I love how you say that, *interesting*, like it's a miracle I turned out okay."

"Okay in the sense that you're creative? Because I bet your parents would rather see you married with a few kids."

"You mean like most parents."

"And not yours?"

"I suppose." I don't know why I felt like I had to deny it. Of course they felt that way, and they were hardly the type not to mention it. *Everything* got mentioned in my family. "What about your parents? How do they feel about the choices their daughter's made?"

"They like seeing me on TV."

"Cyd . . ."

"Well, they do. But . . ." and she paused for a deep breath, "for the most part they've been pretty disapproving. Used to it by now, of course, but they're never really going to accept it."

"Maybe if you brought a nice man home for the holidays."

"A Frosty man!"

"That's right," I said as we both laughed. "A chilled-out Frosty man. Parents love those guys." And who knows, her parents might have liked me. Dayton, Ohio. That's where she was from, and yes, it's always been a mystery, or at least I've always found it so, how remarkable people so often spring from such unremarkable places and families, though I'm not so sure about those families since there must be something about them, perhaps even something genetic, that explains their remarkable children.

11

PARKED IN PALM SPRINGS

There are a lot of RV parks in the Coachella Valley, some of which are quite resort-like both in terms of size and amenities (like the Fountain of Youth), but I stubbornly held out for the Happy Traveler RV Park, which is just off South Palm Canyon Drive in the heart of old Palm Springs. Cyd was not very happy about that when we first pulled in, and it really isn't much, just a few pads, some screening hedges, a little pool, and a small clubhouse/laundry room. But it does have the advantage of being within walking distance of downtown, it's up close to the mountains, and it's cheap. Anyway, I've always liked Palm Springs—how it looks, where it's situated, its interesting history—and I knew it wouldn't take much to get Cyd to come around. Just change Dion's itinerary and I'd suddenly be inundated by an endless stream of interesting bits of local information dredged up from the depths of the Web. So while I did all the hook-ups she set off to reconnoiter our new temporary home. Then she was back, laughing, showing me the photo she'd just taken with her iPhone.

"This is on a bulletin board over in the laundry room." Taking her phone, I turned so I was in the shade. This is what I saw:

The Golden Years
The golden years are here at last
I can not see, I can not pee
I can not chew, I can not screw
My memory shrinks, my hearing stinks
No sense of smell, I look like hell
The golden years have come at last
The golden years can kiss my ass.
Vi '97

"Not very literary."

"No, and you never really get into that, do you, all that aging stuff? How your RVers have all these aches and pains."

"Just like I never mention how relentlessly upbeat they are. Not that I haven't thought about it. Not that we haven't seen that on this trip. But then I'd just be complicating things unnecessarily since they're mostly there as props. But maybe you're right. Maybe I should be more sensitive. Let a few of them develop a bit of depth."

"Right. Wait until we're really fond of them before you kill them off. "

"Still worried about the Gustafsons?"

"Deeply."

Although we were both tired from the drive and getting settled in at the Happy Traveler, Cyd was insistent about having dinner at a place called Melvyn's.

"I've been looking at the map and it's not that far. Just a short walk up Belardo."

"No Uber?" That's what I'd been thinking since there was no way that Minnie was going anywhere.

"No need." She held her iPhone out for me to see the Google map. Yes, there we were down on West Mesquite and there it was a few blocks away up on West Ramon with the Ingleside Inn.

She'd been there before. Actually, she'd stayed at the Ingleside Inn with some friends. She always said that, *with friends*, which meant there'd been a group of them, but all paired off. But I never asked about her friends. I could see that in the arc of her life they hadn't meant that much. Friends like that, they just averaged out, blended together, became indistinguishable. Okay, memorable was not impossible, but you know what I mean.

"You'll like it," she said. "The Ingleside, Melvyn's, very old school, like Musso and Frank in Hollywood."

"Never been."

"But you have been here before, so you know there's not much of the old Palm Springs left."

"You make it sound like we're still in the hunt for authenticity."

But she's right, it is an interesting older neighborhood, tucked away just west of Palm Canyon down towards the bottom end of downtown. It's the old Tennis Club area. And Melvyn's was definitely from another era, both in terms of its menu and appearance—but please, no vegans.

"See?" She was nodding at one of the waiters preparing someone's dinner *tableside*, as they say. "You certainly don't see that anymore."

"That's because you don't see professional waiters anymore. Now they're servers. Wait on me, or serve me. Interesting choice."

"Interesting connotations."

"So what about this?" I was pointing to the menu. *"Frank Sinatra's favorite. Steak Diane."* I lowered the menu to look at her. "Just what is Steak Diane?"

"You wouldn't like it, lots of heavy sauce."

"No?"

"No." Then she reached over to pat my hand. "Try the Coq Au Vin." So I did, while she had some dreadful veal dish smothered in some sort of thick, creamy looking goop. How can people do that, eat veal? But I liked my chicken, and we had a nice wine, an Argentine Malbec (she's crazy about Malbecs), and it turned out to be a nice evening, à la old school Palm Springs.

This is what I said to her over breakfast (microwaved oatmeal) the next morning: "Did you notice that sign for Tahquitz Canyon last night on our way over to Melvyn's?" It was just a block or so up on West Mesquite from where we were staying. "Because I'm thinking this might just be the morning for a short hike, then come back and do a little writing."

"You go, I just want to sit here and drink my tea." She's not much for hiking, I know that now, but that didn't stop me from going.

What a surprise, in most places this sort of thing is on state or federal land, but not in Palm Springs where it's part of the Agua Caliente Indian Reservation. So I walked up to their visitor's center, paid my $12.50, and walked out the backdoor to the trail. Another surprise, there was no one there. I guess I was too early. Fine with me, I enjoyed the solitude and it was a lovely walk, a couple of miles up and back through what would be a fairly lush riparian landscape when the creek flowed. The early morning breeze lifting up off the desert floor, San Jacinto looming way up there to the west, but such a stark contrast between that thread of green and the harsh looking, barren landscape. I'm not sure I'd ever get used to it.

"How was it?"

"You should've gone, it's a nice hike. Maybe I'll come back in the spring when there's water in the waterfall. Get back out to Palm Canyon while I'm at it." I smiled at her. "You were sleeping, weren't you?" We'd both commented on it, how our little Minnie Winnie was such a nice place for a nap, so snug and peaceful. Did Dion ever do that? Maybe he should.

12

THE SMOOTH END OF A COLD SLAB

Back from my jaunt, this is what I wrote, which she then read.

"They'll come looking for us tonight."

"How do they know we're even here?"

"They don't, but what they do know is we haven't left the area. So now they'll start with the most likely places for us to be hiding."

"There are a lot of RVs around here."

"Yes, but most of them look like they've been here a while."

"Maybe we should park over by all that trash we saw." There were several nearby areas that appeared to be unofficial trash dumps.

"No. This is a good spot. Anyone comes poking around, we'll see them."

"And then what?"

He looked at her. What he wanted to say was, well, how did you think this was going to end? You didn't expect to take their money and then just walk away, did you? But that's not what he said. "I'm not sure. We'll just have to see."

"But I thought you said she didn't take their money? Isn't that what Dion told Grijalva and the Feds?"

"I know, but now I've changed my mind."

"But then why's Dion helping her?"

"I haven't decided yet. Maybe Dion's less rigid than he used to be. Maybe he's willing to help someone he might have preferred to arrest."

"Frosty, all these shades of gray. It's not like you."

"No, it's definitely like me, just not Dion."

"Okay, that's got to be them." He turned to her in the dark, just a deep shadow against the diffuse light of their surroundings.

"You sure?"

"Just listen," he said, reaching out to put a hand on her shoulder. Yes. There it was. She heard it. Someone was walking out on the road . . . gravel . . . the crunch of dry twigs. Then he leaned very close. "Like we planned. Wait for me over by the canal behind the RV."

"Dion—"

"I'll be fine," he said, squeezing her shoulder. Truthfully, he wasn't that worried. They'd never expect to run into him out there in the dark. He'd have the upper hand. What did worry him was what he was going to do about it. "Go," he said, gently placing a hand in the middle of her back. Then he waited. Only when he couldn't see her any longer did he turn and carefully make his way over towards the road. A minute later, or maybe it was a bit longer—it was hard, tracking the passage of time out there in the dark—he found it, then he saw their car, just a dark mass against the lighter gravel.

No one was there. Crouching, listening, waiting, looking up the road, over at the trees; it was all very dark and still. Then he heard motion, something in the trees off to his right, like spiky branches brushing against a nylon jacket. Still crouching, he moved quickly towards the sound. Good. They'd never expect him to come up behind them. By now they've got to be asleep, that's what they'd be thinking, so at least they'd try to be quiet, but they wouldn't be all that vigilant. He'd been surprised by that when he'd first started out, how often people just assumed things even when their lives depended on it. It's a natural inclination. We all have it. This tendency to take shortcuts, to leap ahead in our thinking, to assume we understand—but we so often don't. A cop soon learns to pause, to spend a moment or two wondering what the other guy's thinking, only to find out later—and this was always such a surprise, or at least it was at first—that he really hadn't been thinking much of anything.

Pop! Pop, pop, pop. That's what he heard, first one, then three in quick succession.

"Frosty?" she said, pausing to look over at me. "Just what are you up to?"

"Just read," I said, smiling at her.

Now he was sprinting through the trees, both hands holding the gun out in front of him. He'd been too cautious, but they couldn't have reached the RV yet. Then he realized what he'd heard. Those were shots fired out in the open, and close, not over by the canal. Just what in the hell was going on? Then he heard a voice. Estella. "Just stay right where you are." Then he came out of the trees and there they were. Two dark shapes on the ground, another a few feet away, a gun, or at least an arm, pointed in their direction.

"Are they dead?" he asked, closer now, gun pointed at the two men.

"Not yet."

"I thought we'd agreed you'd wait for me over by the canal?"

"They were trying to cut you off." She was lying. He could hear it in her voice.

Next to her now, he held his hand out for her gun. "Well, it's over now."

"Not quite," she said, taking a step back, the gun now more or less pointed in his direction.

"I see. So just how much did you steal?"

"More than enough for both of us . . . if you want it."

"And these two?" and he nodded to the two men at his feet.

"Dion. Come on. You know what needs to be done."

"Wow! She's a black widow."

I nodded. It's such an old plot twist, straight out of film noir. Poor old Dion, blindsided again.

He bent down to check on the two men. One was unconscious but alive, same for the other one, though his breathing was labored. Not looking at her, he said, "So here's what we're going to do."

"And what's that," she said, taking a step back.

"Just a moment." He was going through the men's pockets. Then he found them. Standing, he held them out in his hand. "These are for you," and he jiggled them so she could hear what they were.

"Keys?"

"Which means you've got three minutes to get your shit out of my RV, get in their car, and get the hell out of here."

"Just like that, huh?"

He turned to face her, letting her see the gun. "Would you care to try this some other way?"

"And them?"

"Them?" He laughed. "What you really mean is what story will I have for the county sheriff when he arrives."

"So?"

"Well, Estella, I guess what I'll say is that these two shooters were on my tail and I surprised them out here in the mesquite. I guess they expected to find you here as well, but, well, as you can see, the bitch is long gone."

"And that's it?"

"It is unless I ever see you again."

"Dion . . ." and for a moment he thought she might try to explain.

"Don't," he said. "Let's just leave it where it is."

"And Juan?"

"I'll text Don. Tell him to get Juan on a flight down to Guadalajara to visit his daddy. Tell him mommy's on her way."

"What about Grijalva?"

"Yeah, Grijalva. Well, I guess that's going to be up to me, too." He stared at her in the dark. "Let's go, Estella. These guys can't hold on forever."

"So long, Dion."

"Yeah, so long."

"Is this really how it ends?"

"That's how it ends with her."

"Too bad." She settled back in her seat to stare at me. "You really don't care for Dion, do you?"

"Why do you say that?" But she was right, I'd really come to dislike him. I guess it showed.

"Because nothing good ever seems to happens to him. Because here he is at the end of your unhappy tale all clinically depressed and blue. So I guess that means your next book is going to focus on his psychiatric care."

"As opposed to what, some fairy tale about how he's fallen in love, found a woman he can be happy with, someone who's at least companionable? Well, guess what, maybe that's not how it is for people like Dion."

Now she was really watching me. "Is this Dion talking, or you?"

"It's me talking *for* Dion." Then nodding at her, "And I have companionship, at least for awhile."

"And then what, you'll end up like Dion?"

"Well, who knows?" I said, smiling at her. "Maybe you'd better consider the consequences of your actions."

The Sheriff finally called Gregson, which was the only way Dion was going to get out of this mess. Then he handed the phone to Dion.

"That's a nice story you've laid out for Sheriff Baca."

"It's all I know."

"All you know for sure, you mean."

"You're always free to fill-in the blanks." But of course he knew he wouldn't.

"Not likely. So what do we have here? You were just helping this poor damsel in distress flee some cartel shooters. Shooters you then shot. And why is she fleeing? Because, poor woman, she's inadvertently landed right in the middle of this huge money laundering scheme. How am I doing so far?"

"Very well. I'm actually quite impressed."

"So where is she, by the way?"

"Haven't seen her since Tuesday down in Brawley."

"Where you two split up?"

"Seemed like a good idea, otherwise she just would have been in the way."

"So you knew they'd be coming for her, or you, but you never notified the authorities. Now why is that?"

"If you're referring to you, then you already know the answer to that question."

"Yes, but do you know the answer to that question?"

"Are you trying to get me to say it?"

"There, in front of Baca? Is that what you mean?"

"Seems kind of foolish, if you ask me."

"It certainly would be."

"So?"

"So nothing, other than I hope you'll drop by for a visit. And she really is gone, right?"

"She really is."

"And the money?"

Dion laughed. He'd never been sure about Gregson. "Well, I haven't got it, if that's what you're thinking."

"So it's just Estella?"

"You really think there's someone else?"

"Just making sure there aren't any loose ends."

"Uh-huh."

And that's the way they left it. Baca had his story, and it was Slab City after all, guys come creeping around in the middle of the night a man's got a right to defend himself. Plus, no one died. No, and no one talked, either. Professionals. Got to admire that.

He still had the cell phone he'd taken from the shooter. He was pretty sure one of those numbers was the one he needed. It was, the third one down the list of recents.

"Chuckie! How're you doin'?"

"Uh . . . who the fuck is this?"

"This is your old pal, Dion."

"Esposito. Figures. You take his wallet, too?"

"Damn. Didn't think of that." No, but he'd checked: almost three grand in fifties and hundreds. "But then there probably wasn't all that much, knowing you."

"I'm kinda surprised he's not dead."

"A minute or two more and they would have been."

"Yeah, that's what Chuy said. Said you talked her out of it."

"He heard that? I thought he was out."

"Said he thought you were gonna shoot her, then the two of them. Nice and tidy."

"Sorry. Disappointed?"

"I like tidy, but that's okay. Anyway, guy like you . . . not the type."

"I must have changed."

"Oh, you've shot a lot of women? Never knew that." Then he laughed. "But I bet you were tempted, huh? Bitch made a fool out of you."

"Out of both of us. Gregson, too." He paused, wondering if he should. "But you've probably heard all about that by now."

"Me? Not likely."

No, he could see that it wasn't. So who was it? Well, not his problem. But Grijalva was sharp, he'd figure it out. "No, huh? Fine. Gregson's an ass, but he sure seems interested in your money."

"He think you've got it?"

"Not any more. How about you?"

"No. I know where it is. We all know where it is."

"Yeah, but it's got nothing to do with me. Never did."

"No."

"So I guess that's it."

"I don't suppose—"

"You could hire me to find her? No thanks."

"Afraid she'd shoot you?" He was laughing.

"Never do anything foolish, that's my motto."

"Or at least not twice."

"Yeah," he laughed. "That too."

"So, that's about it."

She leaned back and took off her glasses. "It's good, and I like how *you* tidied up. But I was hoping for a little more."

"Still feeling sorry for Dion?"

"That, and it needs something upbeat. Something to give your readers a bit of hope for poor Dion."

"You don't think that cheapens the story? Throwing in a little sweetener there at the end?"

"Frosty, this is a mystery. An RV park mystery." She put her hand on my arm. "I know you think you're Camus, but . . ."

"But what? I'm just some hack?" Then I laughed. "But so what, right?" And really, I was fine with that if only I could get her to read some of my more serious stuff, but a sweetener really was a good idea, so this is what I came up with, which didn't make her any happier, or at least not at first.

He was a bit surprised by how often his mind came wandering back to the money, not that he ever would have taken any, but the temptation definitely lingered. He was pretty sure she must have salted away several million. It wouldn't have been all that hard to get her to give him a few hundred thousand, but then she'd hurt his pride and there was no way back from that other than a clean break. So was he saying he really would have taken some, given different circumstances? No. Not even if he'd wanted to, which apparently he had if these lingering daydreams of solvency were anything to go by. Oh, come on, he'd never taken her avowals of affection that seriously. Anyway, that sort of thing wasn't for him, at least that's what he'd always told himself after Pris moved out, that some people were just better off on their own—a solo act, only. So that's how he'd proceed—by himself.

He called the Gustafsons and spoke with Donna. Yes, they'd driven Juan over to John Wayne Airport, now he was off to Mexico to stay with his daddy. No, she wasn't that surprised by Estella's duplicity; hadn't cared for her right from the start. But why didn't Dion ever show any of that same interest in the nice ladies she introduced him to? Or were they just too threatening, with all that warmth and understanding and offers of a safe harbor in a tumultuous life. But then maybe he was just threatened by any woman who understood him better than he understood himself. That's what Don thought. He'd even told Dion so to his face: these older gals, these widows of that generation, they'd put up with all sorts of nonsense from their men, not like gals today, so quick to walk out the door whenever trouble showed up, so they were more than prepared to take on a cranky dude like Dion. They'd drag him to the potlucks, make him dance at the parties, let him get drunk with his buddies, disappear over at the golf course all day, no grandkids hanging around, maybe a little dog or cat, assets, for god's sake, but in the end, probably not, not for him.

"I hope this isn't supposed to be that upbeat ending we were just talking about?" I knew it wasn't, that it was just more of the same old gloom and doom. Why? Perhaps because that's how I was feeling, just putting poor Dion in my unhappy shoes. Foolish. There was no way I'd ever be able to hang on to her. Better to just let it go. Better to just let her go since she would anyway. "It feels like you're trying too hard, making it sound like he could never be happy with one of your RV park widows."

"Do you really think he could?"

"Probably not, but that doesn't mean a lesser happiness isn't possible."

"*A lesser happiness*? I guess I'll have to ponder that one. But that's what you think? People settle for a lesser happiness?"

"Don't they?"

"Have you?"

"Well, lesser to some extent, since I'd be happier if things had played out differently, but I'm still happy. It's just a matter of degree."

"So what's an acceptable lesser for Dion? He's already struck out with his wife—"

"And Estella, the black widow."

"Could have been a whole lot worse than a strikeout with her." I smiled. She'd clearly liked that, how Estella turned out to be so duplicitous, a much more complicated figure than at first she had appeared. I'd been taken with the idea myself; that she was a stronger figure than Dion, more complex, harder to figure.

"Yes, but she did like him, she just liked the money more."

"Okay. But I was thinking she was really worse than that, but I suppose my readers will be happier if we just say she was greedy." That's been my experience, that my readers—and most mystery readers are women—prefer the women in these tales, flawed though they may be, to be mostly innocent of those motives that drive men. See, in my thinking Estella was ready to shoot Dion, but that's not how Cyd saw it. For her it was a question of what Estella wanted most, Dion, or the money. So there was that hint of romance even for a black widow. I thought it was just a matter of simple logic. Dion does x, Estella does y, but then he chose z, which meant she was off the hook. Well, in the end these tales are always open to varying interpretations, so Estella can be whoever they want her to be. Now, if she'd actually shot Dion that would have made the interpretation much less fluid, but for some reason—unerring instinct, perhaps—I'd written it just so, or just so they could all be happy even if I was the one who really knew what was in her heart.

"Greedy, or maybe she really needed it." I smiled. You see, there it was, the motive was one we could almost forgive: *she needed it.*

"So there's her lesser happiness, but what about Dion's, because he's still sitting over there all by himself in his RV. Doesn't even have any of that loot to console him. And don't say he gets a cat!"

Laughing now, she patted my hand. "You mean poor old Dion can't even have a pet? Jesus, Frosty, what did this guy ever do to you?"

It was a nice park, close to the beach, though maybe a bit too far to walk. Well, so what? He'd just get a bike like everyone else. As usual, Donna got him involved in the park's social scene, and those seniors did love to socialize. But then they sort of self-selected for that, but still, it just seemed to never end. But it was good for him, Donna was right about that, the distraction, the human contact, the conversations, the flirtations, even those amusing hints of sexual attraction. So maybe he'd settle in for a few months. Why not? A little companionship, and with a woman who'd never dream of shooting him, well, who knew where that might lead.

"So what do you think, right tone? Right direction for your sorry-ass Dion?" I'd finally tried to write something more upbeat, something Cyd would approve of, something to get me off the hook, though it sure felt awkward, like I was starting out on a romance novel, but then that was the very thing that came back to bite me in the ass a few months later.

"Well," and she paused to sniff, her eyes suddenly a little moist. "I don't know what to say. You are serious? Like Dion's really going to meet someone? Even if it's just for a little while?"

"I'm thinking about it. Maybe throw in a pinch of your lesser happiness."

Later, as we snuggled in bed, I told her: "You know, if I'd known what sort of reward you had in mind, I'd have written a much happier tale."

13

THE SHORT GOODBYE

We toyed with the idea of going out for dinner again, with taking a walk downtown, picking out some place at random, taking our chances, but since this was our last night in our Minnie we decided to have a nice dinner at home. Yes, that meant I'd cook since Cyd didn't like to. Honestly, I'm not so sure she even could, not apart from microwaving and reheating and slapping a sandwich together. Okay, she did do omelets. She'd done that for me several times, but no real cooking. Looking at it analytically—psychoanalytically—I'd say this was just another expression of her truncated lifestyle. There just were certain things about living she didn't engage—like anything that smacked of routine, permanence, or domesticity. So we had a nice pasta, a Caesar salad, some garlic bread, some wine, and the two pieces of cake we'd bought over at Whole Foods (all thanks to Uber). It felt very domestic, very comfortable, and she could be like that if you didn't allow your thoughts to stray from the moment. It was sort of like a never-ending Zen dojo, but solipsistic, you know, like there was nothing outside it, outside the walls of *our* little Minnie Winnie.

The next day we backtracked down to Palm Desert, then took 74 up that long twisty grade out of the desert, up and over the ridge through the pines to 371, then the

Anza valley and on to 79 (this time the backside of Palomar Mountain), on to Temecula, and I-15. We made it to San Marcos in good time, turned in the Minnie, which we both missed, paid a minimal excess mileage fee, then spent that night in Carlsbad. It had been a very long day.

In the morning we had a summing up. The consensus: an RV lifestyle can be pretty nice, though it sure helps if you're staying someplace nice. But even when you're not there's no reason why you can't be quite comfortable in your portable little world.

"That's not something you've ever mentioned," she said. "The way you portray it, Dion's RV life looks pretty bleak."

"That's because it is."

"But I don't see how it can be, not with the busy social life we've seen in these parks. You've plopped him down right in the middle of it."

"But that just seems so not Dion, to get involved in stuff like that."

"And this loner business. The no-women world you've put him in." Okay, now she was chipping away at something foundational. He wouldn't be Dion if he weren't a loner, and loners don't have wives or girlfriends.

"I know, but I like to think of him as being more of an existential hero, and yes, I know that's not in fashion these days, though that's never bothered my readers."

"Probably because they have no idea what that even means. To them, he's just this sad, reliant guy. He's got his code. He's got his self-esteem. Definitely the sort of guy you'd turn to in a pinch. But basically he's just lonely, and that's because he's unable to give of himself."

I have mentioned how smart she is, right? Because she was making me very uncomfortable, like she could see right where Dion stopped and I began, or worse, where we overlapped. I changed the subject. "Well, like you read, the no-women thing may be at an end."

"Does that mean Dion's going to be confronted by the demands of a relationship?" She was grinning, and of course I knew why since how was I going to write about something with which I had so little familiarity.

"Well, I guess he'll just have to pick that up as he goes along."

The drive up the coast from Carlsbad was nice. It was a relief to see the ocean again, not that I don't like the desert, on that I agree with Dion, but enough was enough. It was also nice to be driving something smaller. Those RVs are taxing. But what I remember most about that drive was the awkward silence. Really, how is a trip like that supposed to end? We'd built up a lot of shared intimacy and it felt really strange to just shut it down like that. But then she was scheduled to get back to work and I'd be trying to finish *A Cold Night in Slab City*. Her world. My world. So I drove her up to Bristol and then helped her schlep her stuff inside. Back out in the driveway, she held me in her arms for a long time. I felt stricken. She did call me the next day, then came over and spent that night with me, a night together which turned out to be our last for some time, though she's never stayed at my place since.

14

THE PATHOLOGY OF NORMALCY

As they say, there's something to be said for normalcy, though what's to be said remains remarkably unsaid. And in this case it was a tough call. Was it this old life of mine I'd just reentered, or that brief and heretofore unknown normal I'd lived with Cyd? Yeah, well I know which I preferred, but since when has personal preference carried any weight?

Okay, so let's at least finish off that book, the one we'd just spent a week padding out with these great slabs of authentic experience. But I felt very little enthusiasm for that. Sometimes writing about Dion is just a job and I wasn't in a job frame of mind. That wasn't part of my normalcy, new or old, but maybe tomorrow.

It was a bit hard to sort out. Not the end of a relationship. Not really the end of any sort of relationship at all. Yet there'd been something there. Something that had not only occurred, but had occurred in time. The temporal, that's the key human life is played in. Trapped in time . . . living in time . . . beginning . . . ending . . . duration somewhere in between. What you don't want to do is just tread water. But is that even possible? The River Heraclitus just keeps on rushing into the future. River Heraclitus? Man, that *Time Bomb* thing was really weighing on my mind. You do know she's never going to read it? Right?

So the way it went, an hour became several, then an afternoon, then a full day that too soon became a week, then weeks, a month, more months, a season, but I never forgot anything.

15

THEY PAID YOU A LOT

If I were to write this out as a plot summary it would go something like this. Less than three months later he hears from his agent that someone wants to option *A Cold Night in Slab City* before it's even been published. Now who could that be? Right, like he didn't know. So he hears her out, all about her scheme, her production company, his book, she'll star, he'll be hired to help with the screenplay. But what happens, it's a complete rewrite, and now it's this insipid romantic comedy about this misanthropic retired cop who lives in his RV, then he meets this woman who's more than his match. And get this, what little mystery there is just sort of gets thrown in there as an afterthought to give him something to do other than be a character. And *no* significant violence. What the fuck! That's right, it's the Hallmark Channel.

"Who's this guy, Danny, because he sure isn't Dion? And Maria? Is that supposed to be like the Virgin Mary? She's so good, so pure? Poor widow with a son, now she knows her husband was a weak man and good riddance, but here comes Danny, her knight in shining armor. They've completely fucked it up. No one even dies."

"Her husband."

"I don't think drinking yourself to death counts. So what you've got here is a fucking romance novel. I don't write romance novels."

"No, but you helped write a romantic screenplay."

"I didn't know I was writing a romantic screenplay! *A Lesser Happiness!*" I shook my head. "Well, at least that part's accurate. *My* lesser happiness!" Now she was laughing at me, and why not, it was funny, I just wasn't prepared to admit it yet. "I really don't think it's funny, Cyd. Sure, they paid me—"

"They paid you a lot!"

"Right. So I guess that means I'm no longer entitled to complain about what they did to me."

"To *you*? And complain about what? All that good publicity you're going to get? All the books you'll sell? You might, if you allowed yourself, even jump on board and write a few more romance novels, as you call them. Or maybe success just doesn't suit you, like maybe you're more like Dion than you realize."

"Uh . . ." and then I laughed.

"See?"

"That's cheating, you know how I feel about Dion." But she was right. No surprise there since she rarely wasn't. Anyway, we went on like that for some time, or at least until I could no longer pretend to be mad about it. In the end this is what I said: "Well, let's just hope my readers don't desert me, because they'll know who this guy is supposed to be even if you've changed his name. They'll probably feel like I've pulled the rug out from under them."

"It might even be worse than that."

"Not possible."

94

"Sure it is. What happens if they like this new guy, this new Dion?"

"And expect me to write it like this from now on? Is that what you're saying? That Dion's going to be all warm and cuddly?"

"Think you're up to it?'

"No!"

"Poor Frosty," she said, laughing at me. "Forced to choose between losing his readership and his self-respect."

"It's not funny.

"No, but what you wrote was."

"Not intentionally."

16

AMATEUER HOUR

I was groping around in the dark for my cell phone, wondering who'd be calling me this early in the morning.

"Yes?"

"Frosty?"

"Cyd. What's wrong?"

"Something's happened."

"Are you okay?"

"I'm fine, but someone broke in here last night. Over at Lisa's."

"Have you called the police?"

"No."

"Why not?"

"Too much unwanted attention."

"Can't be helped. It's our digital tabloid culture. Rich and famous, just comes with the territory."

"I know, and I agree with you, but Lisa and Terry aren't so sure." Terry was Lisa's producer husband. A decent guy, very successful so far as I could tell, apparently tapped into all that money continually sloshing around Hollywood. But one never really knows. I've never seen a place where people were so unable to get a good fix on what a deal should pay, might pay, and in the end actually did pay. But he *seemed* successful.

"And you're sure you're all right, because you sure don't sound like it."

"I'm fine, but it creeps me out thinking about these guys walking right past my place in the middle of the night."

"Yes, but at least that means they weren't targeting you." I know, why was I sounding like a cop?

"I suppose."

"So at least everyone's alright. That's something to be thankful for. But there's something more, isn't there?"

"Well . . ."

"Come on, babe."

"I was sort of hoping Dion's available."

"Dion! You do know he's just a fictional character?"

"Not so much."

Okay, now I know just what you're thinking, but really, what would you have done?

In the last few years there's been a major flap over a newly discovered and as yet unnamed and little understood lost civilization in the Mosquitia jungles of eastern Honduras. Remote, until very recently impossible to reach, it's in some of the densest of all the remaining tropical rain forests on the planet, but now in the path of the clear-cutters (cattle grazing) and looters. It won't be long before all that can be plundered will be. It's really hopeless since the government, when not corrupt, is powerless to do much about it. What's fueling this, of course, is the illegal trade in pre-Columbian artifacts, something I knew nothing of until I talked to Terry, who, as one might expect, insisted he was just a collector. Was he being truthful? I think so, if for no other reason than that the penalties for smuggling antiquities are much more severe than they are for possessing them, though a huge fine and up to ten years in prison are no joke. But as it stands currently nothing from Honduras can be legally imported, so there's really no way around it, even innocent possession is illegal. Plus, there was no provenance, or nothing beyond the word of the seller, which in this instance wasn't worth much. So the bottom line here is that Terry was legally exposed, which explains why he didn't want to involve the police. It may also explain why he'd been targeted: they knew he'd keep quiet. Ah, but what they didn't know was that I was now on the case. I'm sure they would have been really worried if they had.

"So I'm not sure what it is you expect me to do," I told them. "You admit it was illegal to own it, though you claim you didn't know that at the time. As for the theft, not only do you have no idea who took it, you don't even know who might have known about it. And the guy you bought it from, either he's the smuggler, or he's been working with the smuggler, so there's no good reason to believe anything he says."

"I just want to know what happened. Who's responsible."

"So you can do what? Ask them to give it back?"

"I might. But mostly it's just for our peace of mind."

"So what you really want me to do is threaten them. Tell them you'll let this one go, but if there's any more trouble you'll be forced to go to the authorities."

"But Terry," Lisa said, "then you'll be in trouble for possessing it. And what about all the rest of this stuff?"

"I've never bought anything that lacked proper provenance or was illegal to own, at least not knowingly. At worst, I'll face civil forfeiture."

"But you knew it was Honduran, and you've just told us it's illegal for you or anyone else to import or own Honduran antiquities."

"It's illegal now, or since whenever it was they ratified that treaty, but I was assured this item had been here long enough that it wasn't subject to these newer laws. But then maybe it's true that all of these artifacts should just be repatriated anyway. A lot of people think so."

"In which case you're going to have to give up a lot of nice things? Is that it? But then I suppose that's just one more reason to keep this quiet."

"I know what you're thinking. That it's the money. That since all this cost me so much, to lose it . . . but it's not that so much as it is my attachment . . ." He stopped speaking to look at me. I suppose he hoped to see I understood, maybe even agreed, and really, for the most part I did. Okay, I'm not much of a museum guy, and I'm not that well versed in archaeology, but I could see that he really did have an attachment to them, and so I thought, well, at least they're not sitting in a drawer somewhere. But of course that was an ill-informed and naïve point of view, which I now readily admit. But Terry's a nice guy and he really does seem to love his little artifacts. And then there was Cyd, who seemed to believe that tucked away somewhere in my untrustworthy writer's persona was this other, much tougher guy who found his expression as Dion. Not necessarily your alter ego, she would say, but definitely one of your darker shades of gray.

"And I'd like to know we're not going to have any more midnight callers," Cyd said. Yeah, there was that, which is what I didn't like. And again, just to be clear, I know what you're thinking, that here he is just like Dion trying to save a damsel in distress. Well, maybe a little, but Cyd was no damsel in distress. Ever.

So it was really incredible, here was this crazy family buying up all these Krispy Kreme donuts, and in all varieties though glazed was preferred, then heading down to Mexico to sell them out of the back of their 1978 Ford Econoline van. That's $5 a box becoming $12; clearly an inefficient market just waiting to be tapped by our go-getters. But how is it even possible to stumble across something like that? Like you head out in the morning thinking today's the day I clobber those donuts smugglers? But it wasn't even illegal, you can haul donuts like that across the border all day long. I don't know of any restrictions or tariffs or quotas or anything at all that might concern a van full of donuts. So I guess what it was, they were protecting their racket from competitors. I don't know, maybe I looked like the future donut king of the cross-border trade. Or maybe it was corporate, like they were in cahoots with Krispy Kreme and I looked like unwanted competition. Whatever, they were not pleased to see me.

But did they really have a connection with Terry's missing artifact? I guess that's the important question. And truthfully, I just have no idea, not now, even though it seemed plausible at the time. But then trying to run me over with their van seems like an extreme reaction if all we're talking about are a few dozen boxes of donuts. Yes, but everyone wants to protect their market. Cyd even made a joke of it, saying I was lucky they weren't like the drug cartels, leaving me on the side of the road with a Krispy Kreme donut stuffed in my mouth as a warning. So two cracked ribs, some cuts and scraps, a possible mild concussion, a chipped tooth, and two nights in the hospital, that, and what Terry paid me, was my reward, though that's not quite right since this whole thing brought me firmly back within Cyd's orbit. And I did find out who took the artifact. It was Holmesian logic: pull together a list of who might have known; on that list, determine who had both motive and opportunity; go ask them clever questions; get run over by a van. Dion could not have done it any better, although there would have been significant violence. Actually, if I write about this in one of his books there's going to be dead Hondurans all over the place. So the art dealer, who knew it was illegal, heard from his smuggler pals that there'd be no more unless they could placate the authorities by returning what they'd already taken. They had failed, in other words, to grease enough palms to make it work. To do so they had to make amends. So Terry's artifact, and presumably there were others, was repatriated, only to be sold again, but this time through "proper" channels. I suppose even Terry could buy it (again), though this time there would be no pretense about legal provenance.

"So maybe I'll just stick with being a writer."

"Maybe," she said, smiling at me. "But you did find out who was responsible, which is all you were hired to do. Frankly, I'm not so sure you couldn't do this for a living, but of course you'll need better health insurance." It was amazing now much that little stay at Cedars cost. Thankfully, my employer, and that would be Terry, covered it for me. God, those people have a lot of money. Convalescing at Cyd's wasn't so bad, either.

He did what he'd always done at a crime scene, got out of his car to have a look around. Not that there was always something to see, but it helped to get things situated spatially. Funny how often that proved to be important, how a place felt, its physical parameters, playing some sort of unconscious role in how things went down. But in this case it wasn't much, just a wide residential street gentling curving down from Sunset to San Vicente through a series of graceful roundabouts, flanked the whole way by large, stately homes, hedges, and walls.

He walked up the street looking for that spot he knew he'd find. That vantage point from where it would be possible to sit in a car and watch the gated driveway. What clinched it were the empty coffee cups and crumpled up little sticky sheets of paper lying in the street. Hell, he knew what that meant, he'd been a cop, for Christ's sake: someone had sat there watching the property drinking coffee and eating donuts.

Dion shook his head. It was those fucking Hondurans. He should have known. Doing a little moonlighting. Actually, what this was, they probably owed someone a favor, now the tab was due. That made more sense. They hardly seemed like pros even though they'd somehow managed to pull it off. So now what? Go back and ask again, but this time not so politely? No, they weren't going to tell him anything. There wasn't anything he could say that would scare them as much as the thought of what that other guy might do. Yeah, that other guy, that's the one he was going to beat the crap out of.

"So?" I asked, watching her read it.

"Frosty! I love it. Can I show this to Terry?"

I shrugged. "Maybe, but it's still got a long way to go."

17

WE DO LUNCH

I still had a few loose ends to tie up with the police concerning my *accident*. Really just reiterating what I'd already told them, which was, of course, all a big lie, but then we writers do that so well. Art heist? Donut vendors? Seriously? There would be none of that.

I was with Cyd a lot, or rather she was with me a lot; a more accurate way to describe it. I'm not sure she even noticed, and there was no way I was going to mention it. So she was happy, she was working, she was getting a lot of attention after people got an advance look at *A Lesser Happiness*. She'd been the ingénue, the beautiful young woman, and now here she was in her late thirties this very desirable career woman. Truthfully, women her age, they really are in their prime. No news to me, but now everyone could suddenly see it. So she was doing lunch with these execs who'd put together this attractive package of several more features over the next three or four years. She'd have a stake in it, too, plus a say in how things were done. Yes, but all those details, which is why we were doing lunch at the The Grill on the Alley in Beverly Hills.

I was surprised, The Grill really is in an alley—it cuts between Dayton Way and Rodeo Drive—sort of tucked in there behind Louis Vuitton on the one side and Exclusive Loan of Beverly Hills on the other. Seriously.

Serenely situated between extravagance and that last desperate bridge to fiscal sanity, a Beverly Hills pawnshop, though I suppose the latter is a state most patrons of Exclusive Loan rarely experience. But I'd never been to The Grill. Actually, I'd never even heard of it. Likewise, I'd never been on Rodeo Drive before. Just not part of my world, but then L.A. is a company town and this is where you go if you're in the biz.

Cyd, Lisa, and I were to meet her agent and the execs at the restaurant, an all male contingent, which is why she'd asked me to tag along to help level the playing field. But I hardly recognized her when I picked them up. She is, as we all know, quite attractive, but this was the beautiful Cyd, the one you see on TV. I was a bit stunned by the magic of it, how she could look like that. Just as surprising was the food, which proved to be quite good, though I'd been prepared to be cynical: power lunch, lots of drinks, average food, amiable though condescending and boring conversation. Well, they were condescending, that part proved to be true, and as for all those contractual details . . . so just to amuse myself I sort of took on this tough guy demeanor, which got surprised though approving looks from both Lisa and Cyd. Oh yeah, well maybe you'd better take a look at this guy I brought along. Just try and pull this shit on him! It really was amusing. But what the hell, for all they knew maybe she preferred her men a little dangerous, and who's to say, maybe I really am more like Dion than I care to admit. That's what she's always said, anyway, but Dion doing lunch in Beverly Hills with studio types? Talking over a deal? No, but I was sure taking it all in. No way this wasn't going to show up in one of Dion's books somewhere.

Lisa was laughing in the car, leaning forward to put her hand on my shoulder. "So, you live out here in L.A.?" she asked, parroting what I'd said in the restaurant. "Got some kids in school? One of those private schools over in Westwood?"

"It was just a question."

"Not the way you said it. Like, okay, sure hope they're going to be all right."

"Well," I said, laughing, "he *was* being a jerk. You know," and I turned to look at Cyd, who'd heard this all before, "it never ceases to amaze me how people will do and say stuff that's actually incredibly aggressive and insulting. The way they behave, it's like they believe they've got this divine sanction to do and say whatever they please. Free to indulge themselves with complete impunity whenever the mood strikes them."

"Like road rage?" Lisa asked.

"Yes! Exactly. So you're driving around being this aggressive asshole, but it never crosses your mind to be careful? That you just might be pissing off the wrong person? It's like maybe you just flipped off this sociopath, and now he's going to follow you home and change your whole world."

"So that's what you were doing, being a sociopath?" And now we were all laughing because the guy had just stopped speaking in mid-sentence to stare at me. You could just see it on his face: who the fuck is this guy? Then I gave him a bit of that empty, unblinking stare, the sort that lodges deep within our archaic, reptilian brains.

Suddenly it's fight or flight time, neither of which was a viable option sitting in The Grill.

"No. I just thought—"

"You'd change his world?"

"No, just his tone of voice."

"Well, you sort of did," Cyd said. "Since he didn't have much to say after that."

Grinning, I shrugged. "Sorry. I was just trying to make conversation."

"Uh-huh. *Dion Does Hollywood*?"

"I know, it doesn't really work, does it? My readers will be wondering what's happened to me."

"What's happened to you is you met me."

"Yes, and now I've got all this great material and no place to use it."

She put her hand on Dion's arm. "What is it, babe?" he asked, turning to look at her. "Do you suppose I could get some more iced tea?" So that broke the spell, then he waited to catch the waiter's eye, and when he came over, said, "The lady would like some more iced tea." How absurd. Mr. Solicitous taking care of his lady. But the guy hadn't said much after that, which was just as well since he had no idea what came next if he had.

It's a funny thing about intimidation, how it's got more to do with attitude than with how one looks. Like with him. Sure, he's a big guy, but hardly imposing, yet he seemed to have a knack for telegraphing this unstated though clearly present threat of violence or extreme neuroticism. Not that violence and an unbalanced psyche don't typically go hand-in-hand. But the point was that people usually wise-up and step aside when confronted by someone who's clearly just this side of out of control. That's true even when they think they might actually be able to take them on. But by then there's the very real danger that things will get quickly out of hand. Most people aren't prepared to take it that far, to take it to the next level, plus by now there are just too many risk factors to sort out.

Cyd was laughing as she read it. "Well, that is sort of how it happened, but Dion?"

"Not psycho enough?"

"Not haredly. But maybe you can write it so we see he's just putting on an act."

"Like me, you mean?"

"Well," she said, smiling at me, "mostly, but sometimes I think you sort of like being that guy."

18

NEARING THE END

I was staying with Cyd in Santa Barbara while they were up there filming on location. Another romantic Hallmark deal, this time Cyd was a young widower with two little girls struggling to keep her dead husband's family winery in business (slick, wealthy pursuer; rustic vineyard owner; bitter in-laws). That meant early to bed and early to rise, though what they did for most of the day was just sit around waiting. She said it was boring, and when I tagged along that's sure how it felt.

"Now this is interesting." She was looking at something on her iPad.

"What's that?"

"The difference between fee land and leased land. Ever hear of that?" She showed me the article she was reading in the *Desert Sun*. What it said, which I certainly didn't know, was that half of the properties in Palm Springs sit on the Agua Caliente Indian Reservation.

"So they only lease the land their property sits on?"

"Apparently, and when those lease agreements expire, if they expire, then what they say here is that homes and buildings worth over $2 billion could change hands."

"That's not going to happen."

"No, but it's still pretty amazing."

"It certainly would be. Tearing down all those nice mid-century modern homes."

So this got me thinking about Dion and that RV park where we'd stayed near downtown. Yes, I know Palm Springs is well-trodden ground, threatened on all sides by a ton of clichés (The Rat Pack!), steering clear of that wouldn't be easy, but it's such an amazing notion, fee land versus leased land, your land versus land leased to you by the Cahuilla. But how did this leased land business come about? Is that your question? Because it is an interesting story, one Dion probably needs to know.

In 1878, in an effort to entice the Southern Pacific to build the railroad through the Coachella Valley, the government divided the valley into one-mile squares, granting the railroad every even numbered square for ten miles on either side of the proposed right of way while at the same time allotting the Agua Caliente Band of the Cahuilla Indians every odd numbered square. The result was a vast checkerboard of railroad and Native American lands. Unfortunately, unlike the railroad, the Agua Caliente were not allowed to sell or lease their land, and this was true even after the land had been divided up and parceled out to individual tribal members. But of course they still wanted to, and for all the obvious reasons. Yet it wasn't until 1959 that the issue was finally resolved, the courts (it went all the way to the Supreme Court) ruling that individual tribal members now had the right to lease their land for up to 99 years.

A major consequence of this ruling, one that really needs to be emphasized, is that the cities on the reservation were now free to develop in a more cohesive manner, the courts, in effect, having given the developers a green light. Well, as one might expect, it wasn't long before there were any number of schemes on the part of local politicians and developers to swindle tribal members, though these days it's the tribe (some 400 members) that has the upper hand since many of these initial leases are now nearing the end of their useful lives (most were for 65 years), and in need of being extended or redrawn. As the *Desert Sun* notes: "The longer homeowners and business owners wait, the fewer options they have . . . so landowners, homeowners and business owners are drawing up lease extensions and new agreements one neighborhood at a time." And just how much revenue are we talking about? According to the *Desert Sun*, in 2011 leased land brought in close to $23 million dollars (all administered through the BIA).

A further complicating factor is that many of these original leases now have, or soon will have, fewer than the 35 years left most lenders require to secure a 30-year mortgage. As the *Desert Sun* notes, the result is that "with every year that passes, a home's potential buyer pool shrinks." This has led to a rush by individuals and homeowners associations to "secure lease extensions, which can add up to 34 years to 65-year leases, allowing homes to change hands a few more times." It's this "uncertainty factor," the *Desert Sun* says, that is such a deal-breaker for Palm Springs homebuyers. Also why prices tend to be lower for homes on leased land.

My point? There's a lot of work here for Dion—if he wants it. Leases set to expire, homeowners afraid the land will disappear right out from under their feet, sleazy developers colluding with certain tribal members, BIA corruption, the tribe seeking to buy back land that was previously sold, playing hardball with some of the local business owners over the future of their leases. Well, the list of potential difficulties just goes on and on even though none of this is apparently happening at the moment. But that's fine, this is fiction, I can make of this whatever I want. Like maybe the elderly couple running the RV park where Dion's wintering are having trouble negotiating an extension for their lease. In fact, it looks like the owner of the lease has already agreed to a deal with a local commercial developer to build something entirely new on their land. Then things get ugly when the RV park owners threaten to take it to court. Cyd, of course, insists there's got to be a woman involved otherwise why would he even bother—the core element in her new vision of what Dion's all about—and to some extend I've been going along with that, but I'm worried about my readers. Let's just say he does settle down. That it might even be because of a woman. How's that going to fly? And what happens if we throw in an office and clients and all that boring mish-mash so typical of traditional detective fiction? Yeah, it's a risk. But then there's also a personal side to this—keeping Cyd happy. Dion never had it so rough.

"Jesus, Don, look at that. This was arson." He was staying next to the Gustafsons in Palm Springs. They were looking at the remains of the laundry room/rec room at the park. "You can see where someone used something flammable to get this going. See?" He was pointing to a dark smear of burned wood just below where the roof used to be. "Squirted something up here, then lit it. Burned up into the rafters."

"Charcoal starter."

"Probably."

"What do you think? Tell the cops?"

"No, they'll see it. But . . ."

"But what, Dion?"

"But it's just too obvious. Someone meant this to be seen. Meant this to send a message."

Don nodded. "Like what Sharon was telling us, how someone's really been putting the pressure on to get them out of here." First they'd been told the lease wouldn't be extended, then they were offered a bit of cash to get out early, now this.

"Yeah, well I'd say they just significantly upped the pressure."

As it turned out, the tribal members were mostly in the dark or too scared to say anything. Well, he should have expected that, after all, these were just businessmen trying to do what was best for their tribe. Doing anything more than that wasn't something they'd even considered. But someone had.

It was the plans for that new casino. That's what this was all about. The RV park's location was perfect. So, did that mean organized crime? He knew the BIA went to great lengths to ensure it didn't, but still, this felt much more dangerous than just a few corrupt local politicians and developers. Actually, now that he thought about it he could see that he'd sensed it right from the start, how this was something far more sinister. Fine. So just who were the bad guys? Even more important, what could he do about it?

"Are you really going to have Dion go up against the mob?"

"I know, he's just one guy. Right?"

Now she was smiling at me. "So we're back to Dion the existential loner."

113

"He's got a girlfriend."

"He does? In this book?"

"I haven't written that part yet, but she's there. Or close by. Not that they're living together in Dion's RV or anything, but she's still there in town."

"Uh-huh. And does she survive the book, or just add to Dion's endless tale of woe?"

Now I was smiling. "You're just so suspicious. Well, maybe he's a happy existential loner; happy because he's no longer so alone, and that's all the way to the end of the book."

19

NOTHING GRATUITOUS ABOUT IT

Every town has them, anonymous little strip mall bars lodged in between a Thai place and a liquor store. Hardly worth a notice, way down towards the end of the main drag. In this case out on East Palm Canyon Drive almost to Cathedral City. The Lamplighter. Just a little Tudor style lantern and white stucco, not even a window. Right, an alehouse out in the fucking desert, made no sense at all. So Sheila was to sit at the bar nursing her drink—rum and coke—then text Dion when he got up to use the restroom, but it took forty-five minutes, minutes that annoyed the hell out of Dion, not that he wasn't already in a foul mood. She'd tried to talk him out of it, but he'd reached his limit. This had happened before, back in Philly when he'd still been a cop. Then he'd covered his ass, he and his partner writing up their report just so. Well, sometimes you just lost your temper with these assholes. A few bruises, wasn't that big a deal, but body cameras changed all that. Too bad. Well, guess what, no body cameras tonight.

"So what's this all about?" Cyd asked.

"What I'm thinking, this guy's the local muscle for the mob. He's the one who did whatever it was that's got Dion so pissed off."

"But if Dion . . . he is going to beat the crap out of him?"

"He sure is," I said, laughing. "And in the men's room at the Lamplighter."

"But how's that supposed to work? Because now the mob really will be after him."

"But maybe this guy doesn't get a chance to see who's beating the crap our of him."

"Uh-huh. So this is just a bit of gratuitous violence for your readers."

"Dion's violence is never gratuitous."

"And now you've dragged this poor Sheila into it."

"Shouldn't I? Because when you really think about it isn't she just the sort of woman Dion would gravitate towards?"

"That's not how he seems to me, and it's just so grim, way more ugliness than I'd normally associate with Dion. I wonder if your readers are going to approve."

"What you really mean is you're not so sure they'll approve of Sheila."

"Well, she just sounds so trashy: that name, a rum and coke. I suppose she smokes, too."

"Thanks. Hadn't thought of that. So," I asked, watching her being unhappy, "how would you write it? No Sheila, obviously, or at least a martini. But what about the muscle?"

"I've got no problem with the violence, but this just seems so unseemly. Waiting around to waylay some guy in the men's restroom in a strip mall bar."

"You'd like it better if this took place downtown somewhere in one of those swanky bars?"

"I would, actually. Dion's in there with his lady friend."

"Dion?"

"I know, but she's dragged him there, and then this guy comes over and starts insulting him. Her too."

"Things escalate . . ."

"Things escalate, and then, well, what choice does he have? So then he really does have to beat the crap out of him."

"So now you're the one who's okay with Dion putting the mob on notice?"

"Why not?" she said, smiling at me. "You're the one who has to write it."

"Yes, but following your lead, which means we need to give her a different name. Something with a touch of class, I assume."

"I like Rebecca."

"Okay. So Rebecca drags him to this hipster club downtown somewhere and . . ."

"It works. She's just getting him out of his rut, and he agrees because he wants to please her." She stopped to look at me. "Well, he does, doesn't he?"

"I suppose." I sighed. Poor Dion. Poor me. By the time she was through with us he'd be unrecognizable.

"Dion, who is that guy?" Rebecca was staring over his shoulder at someone.

"The big dude with the man bun?" He didn't need to turn and look.

"He keeps looking over here like he knows you."

"I've seen him around, but I don't know him."

But of course he did know who he was. He'd seen him around with Marvin. Then sitting in the car the morning Marvin dropped by for a chat with Sharon and Bill over at the Happy Traveler. But no way was he telling Rebecca. So far he'd been very careful to keep her uninformed about what was going on. It just wasn't the sort of thing she'd understand.

"He's not going to come over here, is he?"

"I don't see why he should. Why do you ask?"

"Well," and she stopped to smile at him. "He just makes me nervous. Sitting over there staring at us."

Okay. So he understood this game. It's all about intimidation and making the other guy suddenly feel like a stranger in his own life. Like from now on everything is going to be different. And then there was Rebecca. Let her get one whiff of this and who knew what she might do. Well, he'd never had much luck with women. But Rebecca, she was different, or at least she might be. Whatever, it pissed him off. Sighing, he shook his head. Yeah, probably time for something foolish.

"Dion, what is it?"

He reached over and patted her hand. "Nothing, babe." He pushed his chair back a bit and yawned. "That was good," he said, nodding at his plate. "Glad you talked me into it. This is a nice place."

"Too loud."

"Just makes it seem friendly. So," and he looked at her, "time for the check?"

"No dessert?"

"You've got to be kidding."

He waited to get the waiter's attention, then when he came over, said, "That's it for us. Thanks. It was great. So was that wine you recommended."

When the waiter left, she said, "I'm so glad you liked it. Maybe now we can get you out more often."

"You'd like that, wouldn't you?" Of course she would, and there was a part of him, maybe a part he'd never paid enough attention to, which apparently did as well. "Tell you what," he said, "I think I'd better hit the men's room before we leave. I thought it might be nice to take a drive. Be a shame to waste such a lovely evening. But that means you may have to take care of the check if I'm not back."

She laughed. "I knew you'd figure out some way for me to pay." As she laughed he slide the candleholder over near the edge of the table, then when he could let it drop in his lap. It was heavy, a big chunky square of dark brown glass with a fat candle in the middle. Then as carefully as was possible without her noticing, he snuffed it out and wrapped it in his linen napkin.

"Be back in just a minute," he said.

He walked across the restaurant towards the men's room, making sure to pass by the guy with the man bun. He was tempted to say something but he was pretty sure that wouldn't be necessary. And of course the guy was trying to stare him down the whole way. Perfect, he said to himself, you just keep that up, asshole.

He caught a break, no one there. It mattered, since he wasn't sure how this was going to play out. But the last thing he needed was someone else in there to complicate things or be a witness.

He took the napkin and spun it around and around until the candleholder made a tight ball, then took the two ends and wrapped them around his hand before making a fist. He knew it wouldn't be long now.

"Hey, Esposito, who's your lady friend?" That's what the guy said to him when he came in. "Maybe you should introduce us. She's too young for you anyway."

Standing with his back to him at the urinal, Dion said, "You know, we're all going to be a lot happier when you learn to stay out of my way."

"Giving him a little shove on the shoulder, the man said, "Oh, and when's that going to be?"

119

"Just about any moment now, would be my guess." Then he turned and swung the napkin down on the top of the guy's head. He could have done it a lot harder but he was trying to control his temper.

Staggered, the man slipped and fell to the floor on his ass. There were bits of glass in his man bun and all over the floor, the napkin having come undone when the candleholder hit the top of his head.

Bending down, Dion looked into his eyes. He'd be all right.

"So? How're we doing?" he said as he straightened up. "Do I need to call 911?"

"You crazy fucker. You trying to kill me?"

"No, just get your attention. You tell Marvin for me. Okay?"

Back at his table, he said, "Shall we," as he pulled her chair back.

When they reached his car she put her arm under his and made him stop to look at her.

"What?"

Smiling, she said, "Interesting math. Two go in, one comes out."

Smiling back, he said, "One's all that matters."

"So," I said, looking at her. "Better?"

"You know it is."

"And this is a Dion you can live with?"

"I wouldn't be surprised."

20

WHAT WE CAN EXPECT FROM DION

He checked out of the Happy Traveler and drove his RV over to Rebecca's and parked it up at the head of her driveway where it would be out of the way. When he walked into the kitchen she asked him if he felt like he needed to buy a car or would he be comfortable driving her dead husband's old Lexus. In either case the implication was clear: you're done with that peripatetic lifestyle, driving from one RV park to another, taking up temporary quarters as you chase good weather across the American Southwest. "Pete's old car is fine," he told her. "But what I'd really like is an old Vette I can use as a daily driver. Maybe I'll take a look at Craigslist." She smiled. He knew the gentlemen in her circle gravitated towards Mercedes coupes or roadsters. There were old SL 450s all over town. Well, he was Dion from Philly, not Danny from Pasadena. She'd get used to it. "And what about your RV?" He knew she was hoping he'd sell it. He understood. How doing so would be an unambiguous sign of his commitment to her, or to them. "Sell it? I just might," he said. Would he really? That's certainly what he'd been thinking, but that would be a very big step.

"So that's the first way I wrote it," I said as she read it on my laptop. "Then I tried it the other way."

Her backyard was lovely. Nice pool, stately palms, a swath of green grass, a shaded patio with a view of the mountain, which is where he now sat with an iced tea. When she offered he said he wasn't sure. "Not that it wouldn't be nice moving in with you, Rebecca, but I'm sort of used to my RV, and, well . . ." and then he was at a loss for words, or at least he'd run out of excuses. She smiled. She understood. He was like some feral cat she hoped could be domesticated. It was just going to take time.

She stopped reading and stood. "Well?" I asked.

"I like the first one better. There's just no way he'd be that standoffish. And feral cat! Seriously?"

"I know, but I couldn't think of anything else that would be sort of wild and yet liked to hang around hoping for something better."

"Yes," she said, watching me as she chewed on the end of her glasses. "It's interesting that's what you came up with."

"Cyd, it's just fiction. Okay? Just some little story I made up."

"So you always say."

21

TIME BOMB

Rebecca couldn't have been more surprised. Was this budding scholar really Dion? But of course it was that name, and even though she'd wanted to laugh she hadn't. Mostly, that was because she didn't want to deter him, but it was also her desire not to embarrass him or make him feel self-conscious. So off he'd gone reading about Dionysus, then further schooling himself in Greek mythology and Greek history. It was not unlike pouring water on fertile ground. That's how she viewed it. And now there were little green shoots everywhere.

"Well," she said. "Apparently there's just no stopping you. So now we're to believe that Dion, this ex-cop from Philly, has taken up classical culture?"

I smiled. "Everyone needs a hobby."

"Where is it?"

"What?"

"What? Like I don't know what this is really all about." She held out her hand. "Give."

"So I guess this means you didn't like it?" I was pointing to my laptop as I stood.

"Was I supposed to?"

I handed her the manuscript. "I thought it was at least worth a shot. And there's still plenty more. Like how

Dion gets taken with this notion of the Apollonian versus the Dionysian."

"You mean like how you got taken, since that's all I've heard from you for two days."

"That's because I never knew Dion was really named after Dionysus. Not until you told me, anyway. And then I find out he's so Apollonian. All that *noble simplicity and quiet grandeur, only restraint makes the master,* stuff I was telling you about."

"Frosty. Seriously," and she held the manuscript up for me to see. "If you've put any of that stuff in here . . . because if you have . . ."

So that's how I finally managed to get her to sit down and read a bit of *Time Bomb*. No, of course she didn't like it, but that's no reason to think you won't. So here's the premise. It's about this guy who gets fascinated with classical Greek culture. So much so that it begins to seem relevant no matter what he's experiencing. This creates endless cognitive dissonance; a time bomb thrown in his lap.

It begins with the first few sentences of Plato's *Republic*.

> I went down yesterday to Piraeus with Glaucon, Ariston's son, to pray to the goddess, wanting at the same time also to see the way they were going to hold the festival, since they were now conducting it for the fist time. The parade of the local residents seemed to me to be beautiful, while the one that the Thracians put on looked no less appropriate. And having prayed and having seen, we went off toward the city. Spotting us from a distance then as we headed home,

Polemarchus, Cephalus's son, ordered his slave to run and order us to wait. And grabbing me from behind by my cloak, the slave said, "Polemarchus orders you to wait." And I turned around and asked him where the man himself was. "He's coming along from behind," he said. "Just wait." "Certainly we'll wait" said Glaucon.

"So that's one translation, now read this one."
"I'd rather hear more about those mutilated herms," she said, tugging at my zipper.
"Just read it."

The day this whole tremendous affair began, Socrates was returning from the harbor area, accompanied by Plato's youngest brother, a guy by the name of Glaucon. They'd greeted the goddess of the Northerners, those drunken sailors, with a kiss on either cheek and had taken in the whole scene at the festival in her honor—the first one ever! The local harbor residents' parade was awesome, incidentally. And the Northerners' floats, overloaded with half-naked ladies, were pretty cool, too.

Of all the countless guys named Polemarchus, the one who's the son of Cephalus spotted the pair from a distance and sent a kid running after them. "Wait for us!" yelled the young boy, tugging on Socrates' jacket. "Where did you leave your mater?" asked Socrates. "He's running up behind you, wait for him!" "All right!" the guy named Glaucon, Plato's younger brother, agreed. So who should show up a few minutes later? A whole bunch of people, that's who! Polemarchus, of course, the one who's the son of Cephalus, but Niceratus, the one who's the son of Nicias, too, and lots of others, who are the sons of lots of others, not to mention— I bet you'll never guess!—Plato's sister, the beautiful Amantha. All these people were coming from the festival, just like Socrates and Glaucon.

"So what's your preference, traditional, or the one's that's been all tarted up?"

"And if I don't care for either?"

"That's fine, too. The second is Badiou's, by the way."

"I hope it sounds better in French than it does in English. *I'll bet you'll never guess!* Who talks like that?"

"And Plato's sister?"

"Yes, where did she come from?"

"Gender reassignment. One of Plato's brothers, Adeimantus, gets transformed into this sexy new sister, Amantha, though why that was necessary, since Plato already had a sister—"

"Maybe his real sister wasn't sexy enough."

"Well, she was fairly prominent and respectable, this was an elite family, after all. In fact, it was one of her sons, Speusippus, who succeeded Plato as the head of the Academy. But then this is all just ludicrous, anyway, since a woman like that would never have been out on her own. It just wasn't done, not unless she was a courtesan."

"And his real sister was?"

"Potone, daughter of Perictione, who was herself from a prominent family, one that traced its ancestry back to Solon. And this is interesting, or at least telling."

"About?"

"About how these woman lived. So when Perictione's husband died—that would be Plato's father, Ariston—she remarried her maternal uncle, the Athenian statesman, Pyrilampes, with whom she had a son, Antiphon."

"Theirs wasn't the only culture that did that."

"I know. Then Potone's granddaughter married her son, Speusippus."

"Why are you telling me all this?"

"Sorry, I thought you'd find it interesting."

"I do, but why now?"

"Or at all?"

"Yes."

"Well, hang on a minute, I've still got one more thing I'd like to share. Or would you rather not?"

"No, go ahead."

"So this was all new to me, that there's this body of pseudonymous Pythagorean literature out there, and in that corpus there happen to be two spurious works, *On the Harmony of Women*, and *On Wisdom*, said to have been written by Perictione, or by *a* Perictione. Of course, as is usually the case, all we have are fragments." He stared at her a moment. "Now, isn't that odd?"

"That someone would choose to use the name of Plato's mother? A bit. I guess I'm more surprised to hear about this corpus of pseudonymous Pythagorean literature and that a woman allegedly wrote some of it. Do you think that's of any special significance, that these were supposed to have been authored by a woman?"

"Well, yeah, interesting question." The truth was, many of them had been, a truth not widely acknowledged until recently. There were women philosophers? Really? Like that. And Pythagoras was, I learned—learned from her, by the way—not only famous for his inclusion of women, but for his rather liberated view of women, two major exceptions in Greek/Hellenistic philosophical circles.

"And those herms?"

"I knew I shouldn't have told you about that."

"Oh, but I'm so glad you did. Do you suppose the women did it?"

"Whacked them?"

"Because I bet they wanted to. Walking around town, all these big penises starring them in the face."

"I doubt it, though Aristophanes makes reference to it in *Lysistrata*: 'If you're smart, you'll close your coats lest the *hermokopidai* see you.' But this is classical Greece we're talking about, so it's no surprise that the authorities took a dim view of someone mutilating their statues. In fact, some of the perpetrators paid a pretty stiff price for their sacrilege."

"Stiff? Seriously?"

"Well, things were a bit more complicated than I've let on," I said, ignoring her grin. "But you still had people fleeing into exile, property being confiscated and sold at auction, executions."

"Because of a few missing penises?"

She stopped reading to look at me over the top of her glasses. "Herms?"

"Phalluses, on all these priapic statues of Hermes. They were all over Athens. Then one night parties unknown went around and whacked them all off."

"Their dicks?"

"Big—erect—dicks. All standing at attention."

"Uncircumcised?"

"Uh, I suppose. If that's of any importance."

"Just curious. So then she wanted to see yours?"

"Not mine," I laughed. "The guy's in the story."

"That's not you? Because you guys, you writers, never stray far from home."

"Well, this is *very* far from home. I've never even discussed herms with a woman before."

"Makes you nervous?"

"No, but please have the courtesy to stay away from my zipper."

"Really? Because that's a first." Then she reached over and pulled it down. She smiled. "Looks like little herm's feeling a bit cocky tonight."

"That's good. I just might have to use that in my story."

"I want full credit if you do."

"So?" I nodded to the manuscript.

"Just relax, I'll get to it. But why start with Plato? Does anyone even read Plato these days?"

"Probably not, but it's still a famous first line—"

"With who?" She couldn't have looked more skeptical.

"With Platonists?" Then I had to laugh because she was right. No one reads the *Republic* any more, at least no one who's not nineteen and trapped in a lecture hall somewhere. But it really is a famous first line, or so I've read. "I know. Why do I even bother? Right?"

"That's certainly what I'm thinking. I mean, really, Frosty, who wants to read a story that begins like that?"

"So maybe I'll rewrite that part, but keep going."

This is what she read:

From *The Mutilation of the Herms*, by Debra Hamel:

They were statues of the Greek god Hermes, his bearded head perched atop a stone pillar with an erect phallus poking out the front. Ancient Athens was littered with them. They were erected as road markers and placed at entrances to sacred sites and private homes. There were a bunch of them in the Athenian agora (the city's marketplace or public square). There was one at the gateway to the Acropolis. In general, they stood guard over entrances, marking the boundaries between private and public space, between the sacred and secular.

One morning in late May or early June of 415 B.C. the Athenians woke to find that during the night most of the herms in Athens had been vandalized. Then, as now, drunken youths were apt to do this sort of thing, but in this case the damage was too widespread, and the act therefore too organized, for it to be dismissed as the work of a few rowdy troublemakers. From the first, the Athenians took the matter very seriously. It seemed to be a bad omen for the military expedition they were about to launch as well as evidence of a brewing conspiracy against the democracy. A commission of inquiry was established with a view to identifying the malefactors—the vandals were referred to in Greek as *hermokopidai*, literally "herm choppers". In the course of the investigation, the details of another, unrelated offense were uncovered, making things even more alarming for the Athenians, and adding to the body count. Before the whole business was put to bed, several men, at least, would be executed, more would flee the city for their lives, and a major military expedition would be compromised.

So who were these *hermokopidai*? The consensus seems to be this:

That "the herms were mutilated by the members of a single *hetaireia* . . . informal social clubs with perhaps 15 or 20 or 30 members each . . . [which were] a characteristic feature of upper-class Athenian life. The club members—*hetairoi*— shared similar interests and were usually around the same age, perhaps having first become acquainted during their physical and military training as teenagers. They met in one another's houses (a fact that may have served as a practical limitation on the size of a club's membership) to enjoy symposia, drinking parties that could be the setting for anything from high-minded philosophical debate to the less rarified amusements provided by prostitutes. In his dialogue *Symposium*, for example (which was written in the early fourth century but has a dramatic date of 416), Plato describes an evening of entertainment during which the philosopher Socrates and others discourse on the theme of love. But their quiet discussion is interrupted when a drunken Alcibiades drops by with a hired girl on his arm after leaving a less refined party. Depending on the type of evening that was had, a symposium might end in a drunken revel, with symposiasts behaving badly in public, perhaps committing acts of violence or vandalism—the sort of horseplay Thucydides says was mentioned to the commission of inquiry in 415 but that apparently was dismissed as small potatoes.

As for why they did it:

Andocides tells us in *On the Mysteries* that the vandalism was intended to serve as a *pistis* or pledge. A *pistis* was a mechanism by which the members of a group could establish mutual trust. By participating jointly in the commission of some outrage, the members were incriminated equally in the act. Their shared complicity in the offense served as a safeguard against them betraying one another. Normally one would expect a *pistis* to be a preliminary act, a crime committed in anticipation of some larger endeavor for which a proof of trustworthiness was deemed necessary . . . If the *hermokopidai* performed their *pistis* with a view to undertaking some larger act down the road . . . we don't know what it was. The ultimate goal of Andocides' *hetaireia* in undertaking the *pistis* of mutilating the herms may indeed have been sinister, but it's also possible that the *hetairoi* had no immediate purpose in mind beyond cementing the members' ties to the group. The mutilation of the herms, that is, may have been an "unmotivated *pistis*," as Murray puts it. Even if this is the case, however, the vandalism still signified a threat to the democracy on some level. If the bonds linking the members of a *hetaireia* were stronger than those linking the members to the state, and if the interests of the *hetaireia* diverged from the interests of the state, then the *hetaireia* constituted a potential threat to society.

Hamel concludes:

The crime seems to us, 2500 years after the fact, almost quaint, a sort of schoolboy prank, albeit committed on an unusually grand scale. But the Athenians of 415 did not share our rationalistic view of the world. It is a truism to say as much, but in a society that took offenses of this sort seriously, it was a serious offense indeed, and its consequences were grave. The 22 men who were implicated in the crime were either executed or forced to flee Athens, upsetting their lives for years. Most of those who fled were unable to return for more than a decade, until the Athenians declared a general amnesty in 403.

"I know," I said, noting her frown, "but it's such a good story, and she tells it so well, I just thought I'd let her do the work."

"I hope you're not going to footnote this thing?"

"Make it even more awkward?"

"Could you?" Then she smiled at me. "You haven't shown this to your agent have you, because she's going to think you've lost your mind. Plato? Herms? What's next? Or don't I want to know?"

"Well, I was sort of heading off on this tangent . . . Eleusis . . . things said, things shown, things done . . . mysteries, secrets never to be revealed to the uninitiated . . . but perhaps not." Then I had to laugh at the shocked look on her face. "So what can I say? I've got a head full of this stuff, all just clamoring to get out."

"Is it also clamoring to get into print? Because that seems pretty unlikely."

"I know."

"And who's this woman you're inflicting this on? So far she's pretty anonymous."

"My interlocutor?" Blank look. "Like in Plato's dialogues? The person who gets to agree all the time?" I smiled at her. "I thought that might be nice, that there was this woman who did."